Praise for
Bitter Moon over Brooklyn
By Renée B. Horowitz:

"Renée B. Horowitz creates a dead-on portrait of an insular, Mad Men-era world in which women define themselves by their success at marriage...a world in which small acts of malice reverberate. Bitter, indeed, and gripping."

—Janice Steinberg, bestselling author of <u>The Tin Horse.</u>

"The story transported me back to the Brooklyn I remember, and I felt as though I knew the characters personally. The kind of book that keeps you thinking about the characters and the story long after you finish reading the last page."

—Barbara Meyerson, literary critic and Brooklyn native.

Bitter Moon over Brooklyn

A Novel By

Renée B. Horowitz

Clocktower Books, San Diego

Dedication:

To my son, Steve Horowitz, reader extraordinaire.

Fotolia # 71340081 - Brownstone Apartments in Brooklyn © GoodmanPhoto

For the first time in more than 40 years, Marion Davis drove past the Mediterranean Arms apartments in Brooklyn. She double-parked, cut the engine, and stared at the building and its adjacent playground. Flakes of gold-and-white paint peeled from benches and swing sets. The six-story apartment house, its façade once apparently a lovely white stone, exposed traces of orange basecoat. Now, she could see the artificial front of the building—just like the false fronts of the people who'd lived there. If only she'd understood then the difference between illusion and reality before it destroyed her life.

Chapter 1

Marion knew she was pointed out to other Mediterranean Arms tenants: "See that girl—her husband was driving her mother to buy a lamp. They crashed. The husband was killed, but the mother didn't even get a scratch."

The story was told, retold, and exaggerated whenever Marion passed by her neighbors. She could hear the whispers: "So young, so pretty, do you think she'll remarry?"

Marion fled to the lobby of the lovely white stone building and escaped into the elevator, emerging on the third floor. Once inside apartment 3G, she double-locked the door and pulled the chain across for added security and changed into a turquoise housecoat.

In her darkened living room, Marion flicked the remote control from channel to channel until the aching misery her life had become made her pound the sofa in frustration. Her palms struck the carved frame of the elegant bronze-and-white matelassé sofa, but she felt no pain. After a moment, Marion stared again at the television screen until short urgent bursts of the doorbell interrupted her. She used the viewer.

"Stop peeping through that thing and let me in," Sandra said.

Marion released the door chain, locking up again as soon as her friend was inside the apartment. "What's wrong?"

"You're beginning to remind me of an old maid who lived on our street in Syracuse."

"I have to be careful. Everyone knows I'm alone now."

"But you don't need to panic just because another apartment was robbed."

"Another one! What am I going to do?" She pulled at her dark brown bangs and pushed them to the side.

"Take it easy, Marion. No one's ever been hurt. They're just after money and jewelry."

"You don't understand. I imagine all sorts of horrible things. I've never lived alone before—first with Mama and Aunt Lena until the wedding. Then with Alec."

Somewhere along one of the building corridors, a vacuum was running. The sound seemed to echo outside Marion's own apartment, and she was suddenly glad Sandra had come, that she was not solitary for the moment.

"It doesn't help your state of mind to sit around in a housecoat with the venetian blinds drawn, watching television and mourning. A glorious combination." Sandra perched on the curved edge of Marion's sofa, picked up the remote, and turned off the television set.

"That's not true. I was outside for a while, picking up some tuna fish at the grocery, but they're still gossiping about me."

"Forget about those yentas."

"Don't you understand? The best part of my life is over. Today will be exactly like every other day since Alec died. Everything now can only be second rate."

"That way of thinking has lasted long enough, Marion. Even your apartment has a sad air. When someone does visit, it's harder to get in here than into the Pentagon. Peephole, door chain, deadlock. Neil says New York couldn't be that dangerous or no one would reach maturity here."

"I wish I knew what to do."

"Get dressed and come with me for a start. You can't stay home and brood on a beautiful day."

"I plan to drop in on Mama and Aunt Lena later."

"Just the thing to cheer you," Sandra said. She floated around the room, examined a Sèvres figurine, turned off the one dim lamp and opened the venetian blinds before returning to her spot on the sofa. Her blonde hair, curls unfashionably long, looked to Marion like it had never been professionally styled.

"I must see Mama often or she thinks I blame her for the accident." Marion tried to control the quiver in her voice. "God knows it could have been the other way, with Mama dead in the car and Alec without a scratch."

"And you wish it had been like that," Sandra said quietly.

"Don't say that. It's not true."

"All right, have it your way. But it would be healthier to admit you blame your mother for your husband's death."

"Easy for you to say," Marion said, glancing at Sandra's pixie face framed by the long blond curls. "I stood on my terrace last night when you and Neil walked out of the lobby. You seemed to glow under the full moon, a happy couple on the way to someplace romantic."

"We were only off to the movies. A beautiful girl like you could go out, too."

Unwilling to confide her fear of dating again, Marion finger-combed her bangs back into place and looked down at her turquoise house slippers. She said nothing. What did Sandra know of loneliness or fear? She had her husband—the handsomest man in the building. If I had Neil... Marion cut off the thought before she revealed her desire for Sandra's husband.

"Envy won't help; neither will acting the melancholy widow instead of the young sophisticate you used to be. You've got to get out."

"I'm sorry."

"All right, you're sorry. Look, Marion, if Neil and I didn't like you, we wouldn't butt in."

"And I suppose that means you have plans for me."

"We'll talk about it later. Right now, I want to drag you off to A&S or Martin's. I need a new fall outfit."

"But you don't need me."

"My tastes, unfortunately, are plain vanilla." Sandra glanced at Marion's ankle-length turquoise housecoat with the mandarin collar. Her blue eyes sparkled. "With your help, maybe I can find something dazzling."

"Why knock yourself out? Neil's crazy about you."

"Did he tell you that?"

"I can see for myself. He does whatever you want."

"Back home, we call that henpecked."

No wonder they're so happy, Marion thought. Her friend's naiveté added to her charm.

"If I could get you out of this apartment for a few hours, my day would be made."

"Maybe tomorrow."

"It's over eight months since Alec died." Sandra jumped up and went closer to Marion. "Damn shame he was so well insured. If you had to work and support yourself, there'd be no time for gloom."

"Why don't you mind your own business?" She'd never admit the truth about Alec's insurance.

"If I believed you meant that, I would."

Marion tried to change the subject. "What kind of outfit are you looking for? Any interesting ads in the paper?"

"A friend with good taste is worth more than pictures in the newspaper. Come on, Marion, let's go."

Marion felt her resistance crumble. "All right. I'll be ready in ten minutes."

From the bedroom, where Marion brushed her shoulder-length pageboy and put on magenta-colored lipstick, street noises drifting up through the windows were clearer. She heard a shrill voice calling to a child, the distant sound of a pneumatic drill, both suddenly overpowered by the wail of sirens from racing fire engines. It was pure Brooklyn. Alec could have painted this, she thought, translating sound into sight for out-of-towners like Sandra who'd never be part of the city.

Her closet was no longer crowded. Alec's suits had been contributed to the clothing drive of a Yeshiva. Funny for an artist to have had so many suits, but he'd earned a living in the insurance business, painting during the mornings, selling policies afternoons and evenings. They'd lived on a topsy-turvy schedule, exciting because Alec was exciting. In those days, she'd bubbled over with joy, exhilaration that ended with his death.

Marion put on a navy linen suit, just right for late spring in contrast to Sandra, little girlish in pink, and considered how much her friend had guessed. They were very different. The petite girl from upstate was so naive, ready to confide in everyone. Yet she'd discerned the way Marion spent tormented days and nights, walking in circles, unable to sit still or to concentrate. When not shuffling from room to room in slippers, Marion sat by the television, changing channels every few moments because no program held her attention for long. Simple for Sandra to advise getting out more and to hint of remarriage, Marion thought, but the idea frightens me.

When she returned to the living room, Sandra was helping herself to a cigarette, absently fingering the antique case on the coffee table. "That wasn't too long."

"You didn't tell me the details of the burglary. Is it safe to leave my apartment?"

"I doubt if they'd strike twice on the same day."

"Well, better when I'm out." Marion unlatched the door and Sandra waited while she locked the deadbolt from outside with her key and tried the knob. In the narrow corridor, they passed Perry, the janitor, who pulled his vacuum out of the way and continued cleaning the hall without looking up. Marion and Sandra moved along to the elevator.

"Do you think he's the one?" Marion whispered.

"If Perry were the burglar, he'd have retired from work by now."

"Aren't you afraid? You have an empty apartment opposite yours."

Sandra laughed. "Back home, no one locked a door. Anyhow, I think that apartment across the hall will be rented soon. Mr. Fontanna's been showing it steadily."

The elevator door rolled open. Inside, under the crystal chandelier, Mr. Fontanna talked earnestly to a young couple. Newlyweds, Marion guessed. That happy glow on the girl's face could mean nothing else. She looked rather familiar to Marion, like an old school friend. The girl wore a suit, too, but hers was heavy and wrong for the season. Marion felt a surge of embarrassment for her, tinged with sorrow at knowing her own marriage had ended so tragically.

"Will the elevator be free when we have need of it, Mr. Fontanna? We must pay the moving van by the hour." The girl's accent was hard to place.

The boy's face turned red. "It will be great living right across from Sheepshead Bay."

"Oh, but what a street to cross. The traffic in Brooklyn is fierce."

"Live in New York long enough, you get eyes in back of your head."

"We assign a time to move into the Arms," Mr. Fontanna explained, "so the janitor takes up the carpeting and pads the walls in one elevator."

The girl glanced down, as though noticing the broadloom for the first time, then quickly looked from her husband to the renting agent without speaking.

"I'll give you some free advice," Mr. Fontanna said, bushy eyebrows dominating his thin face as he smiled at them. "My boy Joey's still single, but I know what it's like for young people just starting out. Here's what you do. You tell those movers you want a flat rate. They'll claim they don't give flat rates, but you can reach an understanding. You know what I mean?" He gestured, rubbing thumb and first two fingers together.

Sandra won't have much in common with neighbors who count every penny, Marion thought.

When the elevator doors slid open, she lingered in the lobby, admiring its Mediterranean style furniture as she always did, and gave the couple time to leave the building first. Before their wedding, she and Alec also had checked the new buildings, but rental costs meant little to them. Apartments blurred together in an endless mass of thinly partitioned boxes until Marion saw the glamorous lobby of the Mediterranean Arms and knew this was the place. Despite Alec's observation that they weren't going to live in the lobby, Marion had quickly furnished their apartment with similar Italian and Spanish pieces.

Sandra took Marion's arm and glanced towards the young couple who were now standing outside the building in conversation with the renting agent. "Those gossipy women who roost in our playground will slaughter her. No money. Probably half their income will go toward the fancy rents here."

"She looks so happy. Why do newlyweds glow and the older women wear bitter faces?"

"Ah, don't you know? I guess you weren't married long enough."

In the September sunlight, the white stone façade of the six-story building glittered. Across the street, Sheepshead Bay had an empty weekday air despite sailboats and motorboats dotting the green-blue water. Marion and Sandra walked leisurely toward Ocean Avenue for the bus and nodded to neighbors as they passed the playground next to the Mediterranean Arms.

They waited without talking. Marion started to reach into her handbag but remembered she had three twenty dollar bills. By the time she asked Sandra for change, the bus had turned the corner.

"Just get on; I'll pay for both of us."

Marion slid into a window seat and watched the Avenue speed by, enjoying glimpses of uniformed doormen and richly decorated lobbies as they passed other new buildings.

"I still think ours is the most glamorous one in Brooklyn."

"That's what their advertisements say, but it's just an illusion. Neil says if management had used a marine motif and called it Sheepshead Arms instead of Mediterranean Arms, half the apartments would be vacant."

Leave it to Neil to think of that. He's so original. Marion started to say that aloud but decided Sandra might construe it another sign of jealousy.

They changed buses and settled down again. More new buildings. Someone pulled the cord, sounding the buzzer as the bus approached Prospect Park and Marion imagined it was Alec. In another moment, he would gather easel and paints, grinning at her as he pulled a black beret from his pocket and covered his short chestnut hair. The beret, he said, was protective coloration. Some of their nastier neighbors called it an affectation, but Marion knew he couldn't wait to change from dark business suit to knit shirt, chinos, and beret. Without the beret, he still resembled Alec Davis the insurance salesman, which was the reason she'd once urged him to grow a beard.

"I can't remove a beard on the job, sweetie."

"But painting is your real work."

Alec had winked at her and planted the easel in front of the lake at the spot where he tried to capture water and rowboats through a huge curved branch. The branch had been painted in first and framed the canvas; he'd never completed the scene. Of all his paintings, he'd sold only one, a Rabbi wearing his prayer shawl, an ugly portrait that Marion disliked. Sometimes, she clutched his paintings and sketches from the closet and admired them, but the crying spell that followed was less endurable than emptiness. Alec the artist and the glamour attached to him, as well as Alec her husband, had been lost and so had Marion's belief something special was about to happen to her. I'm only twenty-five years old, she reminded herself. Surely there'll be more to my life than this. She tried to erase the sudden image of Neil's dark eyes that more and more dominated her thoughts and visualized Alec instead.

The buzzer sounded again and Sandra moved into the aisle. Women crowded towards the doors, separating Marion from her friend. Suddenly she dreaded being left alone and surged out of her seat into the human tide. It was crowded all the way to Hoyt Street, where they ducked through revolving doors into the first department store.

"Going out among people has revived you," Sandra said.

"I was thinking about Alec. He loved crowds."

"My brother's like that, too."

Marion stopped before the bank of elevators and inspected the other girl, who calmly stared back at her, blue eyes challenging Marion's gray ones; she was annoyed at herself for turning away first.

"Basement elevator. Going down."

"Let's wander through the basement and see what's on sale," Marion said.

Just beyond the elevators on the basement floor, women gathered around a display table, pushing against each other. Neither one could see what was offered at the table, obscured by reaching, shoving shoppers, but Marion stopped to watch.

"Can you see?"

"Don't be silly. Let's get out of here."

"Wait a minute. It must be a special. Something I can bring to Mama."

"She can do without another guilt offering, Marion."

"I've got, I've got," a woman in front of them cried and pulled her hand back over the circle of shoppers. "Oh, hell, cream color."

"I'll take them," Marion said.

The woman passed along what was in her hand.

"Thank you."

"Go jump in the lake. I wasted half an hour." The woman hurried away, mumbling to herself.

"What's with her? She didn't want it."

Sandra's face had turned pink. "If you really need that, pay for it and let's get out of here."

"I don't even know what I ... It says hand-edged. Twenty-nine cents." Marion held them out as they walked towards the cashier. "That's a steal, handmade placemats for twenty-nine cents."

"Hand-edged."

"It's still a good buy."

"If you want it and can use it, then you have a good buy."

"Sandra, you're wise beyond your years."

"It runs in my family."

"Now don't spoil everything." Marion paid for her purchase and started back to the elevators.

"I've told you that Eddie moved down from Syracuse, and I want you to meet him."

"I figured you were leading up to your brother and me."

"You're too damn stubborn. What makes you think I'm matchmaking?"

They were in the elevator again now and remained quiet before the other passengers. Marion rolled the top of her package, crushing the paper bag. "If not matchmaking, what do you have in mind?" she asked as soon as they were alone. "Is the sophisticated widow supposed to have an affair with her best friend's brother?"

"I understand your cynicism, but for once forget the past and try to enjoy life again."

"Exactly what I try not to think about."

"Why?"

The question, flat and unexpected, forced Marion to face her fears. "Because I'm unbearably lonely and my desires have been suppressed for months. If I let them come to the surface, I'll lose control of myself completely."

"It's worse to have no future."

"Should I sleep with the first man who's kind to me? Drift in and out of affairs until I get tired of that and marry some boor?" She turned to Sandra. "Would that be better?

What do you want from me? Can't you see I'm all mixed up?"

"Come to dinner Saturday night and meet Eddie. That's not like a real date, so if you don't want to see him again, you can let it drop."

Marion hesitated, seeking a way out. "What does he do?"

"I told you a few weeks ago that Eddie just finished his Ph.D. thesis."

"But what career is he planning?"

"He was on a teaching fellowship. Now he'll be teaching Spanish literature."

"A teacher!"

"What's wrong with that? Alec was an insurance salesman."

"Alec was an artist."

Sandra walked over to the Town Shop and started sliding dresses along the rack, glancing at each one for a moment before pushing it away.

"If I'm going through the inferno of circulation, meeting men, dating them, I want someone exciting," Marion said. Like Neil, she thought.

"But what can you tell about anyone until you live with him?"

Marion pulled out a sapphire blue shirtdress and held it up far Sandra's inspection. "What about this? It will be perfect with your coloring and only $24.95."

"Twenty-five dollars is too much for that dress. I'd rather spend less and buy something for Toby with the difference."

"I guess I have become pretty self-centered," Marion said. "I didn't even ask how Toby is today."

"It was only another cold, not tonsillitis. He's back at nursery school."

Sandra had three dresses over her arm and Marion followed her to the dressing rooms where she waited while a saleslady fussed with hooks and zippers. She agreed with Sandra that Neil would like the blue polyester one.

"That color matches your eyes perfectly," Marion decided, staring at her friend. Sandra, with her curly blonde hair and big friendly smile, looked like a high school cheerleader or the girl next door—familiar from so many movies.

"Shall we lunch downtown?" Sandra asked while her dress was boxed.

"Why not?"

Sandra's face glowed. Marion realized she'd atoned for her rudeness. Impulsively, she turned to her friend. "If your brother's as good-natured as you are, I'd like to meet him."

"Eddie's much more pleasant than I am. I think you'd be good for each other. He went through a rough experience recently," Sandra said. "Not as bad as yours, but rough for him."

She found it hard to show an interest in Sandra's brother, so Marion kept still. The troubles of others no longer interested her; they didn't lessen her own pain.

During lunch, Marion found herself giggling once or twice at Sandra's comments on the Brooklyn scene. She even agreed with Sandra that all this was pretty remote from the Broadway columnists' view of the same city, although in her heart, Marion visualized herself as one of the beautiful people.

"Where to?" Sandra asked after they divided the check.

"We may as well take the bus back. I can get off at Beverly Road to see Mama."

"Don't go there now. It will spoil the only good day you've had."

"I must."

"You can't let yourself drift this way, Marion."

"I know it!"

"Then take control again. Get the guilt you feel for blaming your mother into the open. If you can't talk to her, talk to your aunt."

"I'll try. But it will be like this for as long as Mama and I both live."

Thinking about that long-ago day now, Marion marveled at the low prices then and the difference in people's lives when crime was rare and women were 'girls', who thought they needed a man to be happy.

Chapter 2

When Marion arrived that afternoon, the hallway and living room of Bertha Benjamin's apartment were dimmer than her daughter's had been. An older place, where paint and furniture predated off-white and pastel-oriented decorators, the apartment always seemed dark and shabby. Marion was thankful that none of her neighbors at the Mediterranean Arms had ever seen this place.

Her mother, short and stout with yellowish white hair instead of the blue rinse Marion used to urge on her, answered the doorbell.

"How do you feel today, Mama?" she asked, trying to put some warmth into her voice.

"Thank God."

"Mama, why don't you ever answer the question?"

"And what should I say? If I am better than last week, I thank God and if worse, I am thankful not to be sicker."

If only she said it with a twinkle in her eye or a smile, Marion thought, watching as her Aunt Lena entered the room.

"Sit down, Marion. Put your feet up on the hassock. I will make some tea."

"She is not an invalid."

"Aunt Lena enjoys fussing over me, Mama."

"You should be the one in the kitchen making tea for your mama and aunt."

They had nothing to say to each other before Aunt Lena returned with the tea and cheesecake on a small wooden tray. She was taller than Marion's mother, thinner and Americanized. Unlike the mother who always wore housedresses with buttons down the front, the aunt had a variety of pretty dresses and her hair, dyed red, was in a fashionable upsweep. Both sisters emigrated from Germany nearly thirty years before, but only the younger mastered the new language and the new customs. In Marion's childhood whenever mores of the new world were in conflict with her mother's old world background, Marion depended on Aunt Lena to intercede for her. When the lipstick question arose in Junior High, Aunt Lena and Marion were victorious, but there were many compromises, some worse than outright defeat. On Open School Nights when both women visited her classrooms, she always hoped the teacher would mistake aunt for mother.

"Marion, that cake is milchig," her mother said. "What did you have for lunch?"

What did she have for lunch? She couldn't tell Mama she'd eaten nonkosher hamburgers. Now she'd compound her blatant disregard for the Jewish dietary laws by eating the dairy cake.

"I went shopping with Sandra Kramer. This is for both of you." Marion held the package out towards her aunt.

"You did not answer the question. I know, I know. You and that friend of yours were so busy in the stores, you never had time to eat."

"Leave her alone, Bertha. She can take care of herself," Aunt Lena said.

For a moment, as Marion caught the glance Aunt Lena directed towards her mother, she shivered, expecting one of them to break the self-imposed barrier, to talk about the accident that killed Alec. Her mind leaped ahead to the scene that would follow. It would be better to talk, Marion thought, but I can't do it.

Mama had telephoned so often asking Alec to run her errands. That rainy day, she called up and asked him to drive her out to Long Island. "Just to buy a lamp." Alec was dead because Mama wanted a new lamp.

Marion bit her lip but couldn't keep from looking around the living room for a brass Empire lamp. It wasn't there. As often as she'd been to this apartment without seeing it, she still searched, unable to convince herself Mama had never picked up the lamp later, after she'd recuperated from her stroke. Marion sighed, sipped her tea, and toyed with the cheesecake Aunt Lena had cut for her.

"She took the little boy along?"

"Who, Mama?"

"Mrs. Kramer. Your friend. She took the little boy along or again a babysitter?"

"A babysitter , I guess."

"What kind of mother leaves her boy and runs all the time?"

"All the women do that, Mama."

"This is not the old country," Aunt Lena said. Marion had heard her aunt speak those words in her defense hundreds of times but Mama never paid attention. Even now, halfway to the bedroom to answer a ringing telephone, her voice soon filtered back to them. Marion knew she'd be engaged in an interminable conversation. This was her opportunity to talk to Aunt Lena, but she didn't know where to begin.

"You have some color in your face today."

"I'll survive."

"Don't worry, Marion. We are a strong family, but I want more than survival for you. With your Mama, if a person eats well, that's enough but I'm waiting to see your eyes sparkle again."

"Mama is my real problem." Marion followed a loose thread on the old brown sofa with her fingernail.

"Tell me something new."

"All right, it isn't news to you but I can't wrap my whole life up with Mama's only to show I don't blame her for killing Alec."

"For killing Alec," Aunt Lena echoed. "Is that how you think of it?"

Marion looked down at the worn carpet. "She called up; she said, 'Alec, you will do me maybe a favor' and he went and I never saw him alive again."

"And that's Bertha's fault?"

"She never even liked him, but he was good enough to use as a chauffeur."

"Your mother suffered, too."

"Aunt Lena, I can't go on this way."

"Then find another man and live in the present."

"I don't want just anyone—to have children and sit around in the playground like the other women, each day the same and two weeks in the Catskills every summer. I want to marry someone who can take me to Hawaii or Paris maybe or some other glamorous place." Or South America on his business trips with Neil, she thought.

"Does that matter? You go out, you meet a nice boy, you marry him, you have someone to sleep with again, and you won't be so lonely."

Marion looked over her shoulder to see whether Mama was returning. "I don't care anymore."

"You haven't been near young men all these months."

Bertha Benjamin came into the room. "Marion, Cousin Natalie's daughter, the one who just got married in Miami Beach, is moving into your building."

"Of course, the girl in the elevator."

"On the fifth floor, a nice apartment but without a terrace. Ah, I will not have to worry so much that you are alone." Her mother sat next to Marion on the sofa and for a moment, the girl thought she'd try sympathy and steeled herself.

"I told you not to worry, Mama. If I get nervous, I call the Kramers and either Sandra or Neil comes down."

"And that's another reason why you should marry again," Aunt Lena said.

"Marry again? Who said anything about that?"

"When you and I were widowed, Bertha, we accepted it, but Marion needs a husband."

"You are wrong. Marion does not think of this."

"Stop it both of you," Marion shouted.

"She will want to marry and have children. You must not stand in her way."

"I am not inhuman, Lena. I would welcome him as I welcomed Alec," Bertha Benjamin said.

Is that what I'd face again, Marion asked herself, remembering her early dates with Alec and her mother's reception of the artist.

"Marion, someone is at the door for you."

She would find that the door had been closed and Alec, short chestnut hair wet from a rainy evening, left standing in the hall. She'd run to the door and pull him in.

"Come and talk to Aunt Lena while I get ready."

Passing her unsmiling mother to Aunt Lena's room was a difficult walk for both of them, but Aunt Lena always greeted Alec warmly. "How is the painting? Did you finish the seascape?"

"Too windy at Rockaway today."

"So next Sunday will be better."

When Marion was ready, Aunt Lena went as far as the door of the apartment where Bertha Benjamin did sentinel duty.

"Let them sit here and watch television tonight," Aunt Lena said. "Alec doesn't have to spend all his money at the movies."

That would be great, Marion thought. Spending the evening in the living room with Mama. She implored Aunt Lena with a quick look.

"And you and I will go to the movies."

"You are crazy, Lena."

"Get your umbrella. We need an outing."

Marion leaned against the door and knew her mother
didn't trust them enough to go but, rude as she was to Alec,
she couldn't say so. Make her go, she prayed silently to Aunt
Lena.

"Come, Bertha."

"The boy goes home at eleven."

"Okay, Mama."

The door closed behind the two older women and Marion
took a deep breath. She heard Alec's laugh. "I thought it was
pretty grim," Marion told him.

"Not that bad, sweetie."

"If Mama doesn't become more human, I don't know
what I'll do."

"You know you love her."

Marion was quiet. Without realizing it, Alec had
answered her complaint the same way Aunt Lena always did.

"How about coffee?" Alec asked. "And didn't you tell me
you had a chess set?"

"I have a set, but I don't know anything beyond the
names of the pieces." Marion looked at Alec to see how he'd
react to her admission. Why had she told the truth to the one
she most wanted to impress? Now he would consider her
stupid.

"I'm too lazy tonight even to teach you the basics. What
about gin rummy instead?"

Marion kept the deck of cards in her room. "Wait here,"
she said in deference to Mama, but hoped Alec would come
after her.

He was so unlike others she'd dated, the ones who'd
never have missed the chance for heavy petting afforded by
the empty apartment.

Marion lingered in her bedroom, giving Alec plenty of
time to get the idea. Not that she wanted him to try to go too
far, but he was so good-looking with his broad shoulders and
dimpled chin—and he was an artist. She'd been crazy about
him ever since they'd danced at a little nightclub on the
Island, as they called Long Island.

He hadn't moved from the kitchen; she had to go back. What would her friends say if they knew she'd spent a date with Alec Davis playing gin rummy? Their criticism would be balanced by admiration of Alec as a good catch. "Don't let this one get away," one of the girls had said.

"Do you always shuffle the cards that way?" Alec asked at her turn to deal.

"Isn't this the right way?"

"It's cute. You look like a professional gambler."

No one had ever called Marion "cute" before. Sexy and sophisticated were the usual compliments, ones she aimed for. "That doesn't sound very glamorous."

"You're too sweet for the phony stuff," Alec said. "Oh it's all right to put on an act for laughs, but you have to know it's all a big joke and not take yourself seriously. You have the slinky dresses and I have a beret."

Marion wondered what he was talking about. "I loved it when we went to the Palisades last week and you wore your beret. Did you sell the painting yet?"

"Marion, Marion. No one will buy that sketch of the New York skyline. It's been done over and over again."

"I like it."

"It's great to have an admirer. I'll give you the sketch and you can start an Alec Davis collection."

"Really!"

"Sweetie, does it mean that much to you?" He sat on the edge of the kitchen table and looked down at her.

"I think it's the most exciting thing that ever happened to me."

"If I painted portraits instead of landscapes, I'd love to capture your irresistible combo—dark hair with lighter highlights and smoky gray eyes."

Marion gazed at Alec and wanted to tell him that she loved him. Obviously, despite his words, he couldn't care much for her for he suddenly stood, ready to leave.

"It's nearly eleven."

"Mama won't be back for a while."

"She made it quite clear that 'the boy goes at eleven.'"
Alec put his arm around Marion and drew her out of her chair.
"Let's sit in the living room for a few minutes."

Without turning on the lights, Marion and Alec sat down
on her mother's massive brown sofa. Alec kissed her and
Marion felt giddy with happiness at being so close to him. He
held her without speaking and kissed her again.

"You're the only girl for me," he said. "When are we
getting married?"

I must remember every second of this night, Marion
thought, and looked at Alec in the sliver of moonlight that
came through the venetian blinds. His face was serious now
but laugh lines around his mouth contradicted the solemnity.
Marion leaned toward Alec and kissed him by way of an
answer. Too late, she realized that the door to the apartment
had opened and turned to face her mother and Aunt Lena.
Nervously brushing strands of her dark brown bangs into
place with her fingers, she tried to seem composed.

"Two bums who cannot be trusted."

"Mama, Alec just...

"Mrs. Benjamin, I...

"Wait a minute, Bertha."

They attempted to reason with Marion's mother, but she
flung her arms in all directions, silencing them. 'Come to the
movies, Bertha.' 'Yes, Mama, go to the movies.' So I went
like a fool and left the artist bum to sleep with my daughter."

"What are you saying, Mama? Stop!"

"Every light off. I find them on the couch with every light
off."

"Mrs. Benjamin, we were playing cards all evening."

"Get out from my apartment."

Alec looked at Marion.

"It would be better for you to go," Aunt Lena said. "I'll
calm my sister."

With one backward glance to see whether he could help
Marion, Alec left, while Marion wondered if she'd ever see

him again. The swift transition from the fulfillment of her hopes to her mother's accusation had left Marion numb.

"A girl from a good Jewish family does not spend the night with a boy in a dark apartment," Mrs. Benjamin shouted.

"We didn't do anything wrong, Mama. Please don't be so unreasonable. Alec and I are engaged."

"Engaged. So, that gives you a right to disgrace your family?"

"Don't speak that way to the girl," Aunt Lena said, thrusting her slim figure between mother and daughter.

"And what do you know? If I had not listened to you in the first place, we would be better off now."

"Marion says they did nothing wrong."

"There is one way to find out."

"Mama, I tell you..."

Mrs. Benjamin seized her daughter by the arm. "Come. We will know the truth."

Aunt Lena ran out of the apartment after them. "Bertha, where are you taking the girl?"

Without waiting for the elevator, they rushed down the stairway to the ground floor, Marion screaming aloud when they stopped in front of Dr. Saul's apartment-office.

"It is eleven-thirty at night. You can't wake a doctor except for emergencies," Aunt Lena still tried to stop her sister.

"An emergency, this is."

Dr. Saul answered the doorbell, his face incredulous as he listened to Marion's mother.

"Don't pay any attention, Doctor. My sister is a madwoman." Aunt Lena turned to Marion. "We will go home now."

"Marion will stay here until Dr. Saul examines her."

"We didn't do anything." Marion sobbed with shame for the scene they were enacting in front of a stranger as well as for her own predicament. She would not live with that hysterical woman another day, she vowed.

"The examination will take just a few minutes... I'm sorry, but I think it's the only way to calm your mother," Dr. Saul said.

Marion followed him into his office, and crying so hard that she could barely hear his instructions, got onto the examining table and put her feet into the stirrups. This could not be happening; it was a nightmare, she thought, while she tried to forget that now Alec would probably never want to see her again.

In a moment, the examination ended and the doctor returned to his waiting room. Marion covered her face with a handkerchief and followed. A horrible fury had replaced her helpless despair. I'll always hate you for this, Mama, she repeated over and over to herself.

"Your daughter told you the truth," Dr. Saul said coldly. "With your sick ideas, you've committed an injustice against her."

"Did Marion ask you to say this?"

"For God's sake, have you no sense at all?" Aunt Lena shouted.

"Mrs. Benjamin, if you don't trust your physician either, why did you come to me?"

"I am sorry, doctor. I was excited."

"With your high blood pressure, emotional outbursts are a luxury you simply can't afford. Now when you get upstairs to your own apartment, I want you to take this sedative." Dr. Saul handed Marion's mother a small envelope.

"All right, doctor."

"You had a checkup last month and I warned you then not to get upset."

This was news to Marion and she lowered the handkerchief for a moment, but everything that had happened this evening following Mama's return from the movies came back to remind her that she didn't care about her mother anymore. Let Mama take care of herself and leave me alone, Marion thought bitterly.

"You had better get some rest now," Aunt Lena said to her sister and took her by the arm.

"Yes, yes."

Marion, suddenly alarmed at her manner, saw that all the fight had drained from her mother. "Mama, come upstairs and lie down."

Mrs. Benjamin went meekly. From that night on, although she never apologized, she modified her attitude towards Alec, and Alec seemed to like her. After the marriage, he was the one who urged Marion to visit her mother more often. Mama no longer called him "the artist bum" but introduced him to her neighbors as "my son-in-law, the insurance man" and Alec never corrected her. It used to annoy Marion that her mother refused to understand Alec was an artist and only sold insurance because he had to do it. Eventually, Marion remembered now, her own bitterness had faded until the automobile accident brought it all back. She thought about those early days and knew that she couldn't stand another courtship under her mother's eyes.

Now, remembering when Roz Geller moved into the Mediterranean Arms, Marion regretted her indifference toward the young refugee. She hadn't known then of Roz's defense against the malicious plots of other neighbors.

Chapter 3

Although Roz Geller had hoped for a traditional American honeymoon at Niagara Falls, the new apartment with its high rental interfered with that dream. Marty explained patiently that Niagara Falls was not the honeymoon site it once had been, except in the movies. Only shnooks from the Midwest went there now. People he knew honeymooned in Bermuda or Miami Beach and they had met in Miami. Only Lakewood, New Jersey, was within financial reach, so they might as well spend the five days they had in Lakewood.

Roz listened carefully nodding her head, hair just a few shades darker than her cousin Marion's, but with a center part. She'd willingly do whatever Marty wanted even before he explained.

After their short honeymoon in Lakewood, Marty returned to work and Roz had little to do but neaten the apartment and dust the double dresser and night tables of their bedroom set. When they moved into the Mediterranean Arms, they had only a new oak bedroom set and whatever odd pieces of furniture Marty's family could spare. Roz, who didn't mind waiting indefinitely to furnish the place, hoped Marty would soon get over his impatience with their empty living room.

She felt guilty for not contributing to the expense of the luxury apartment but kept her feelings to herself. Despite his tough manner of speaking, Marty was a tender husband who insisted Roz stay home now and take it easy. "I know you worked every afternoon after school for years." Her father, a waiter in a small Miami Beach hotel, didn't earn much and Roz's salary helped keep the family going. As refugees they'd survived just as they'd survived long before her birth when the family fled Germany for Cuba.

The Mediterranean Arms was far from that life. Roz held her breath when the agent told Marty what the apartment rented for, almost two weeks of his take-home pay. When they left the building that day, Marty took her hand and pressed it tightly. "Who said I couldn't afford to get married? Wait until the fellows at the office see this place."

"Are you sure it is for us?" Roz asked timidly.

"We'll have to give up a few things, but it'll be worth it."

"Maybe a cheaper..."

"Look kid, in this city you've got to put up a big front or they'll walk all over you. That's the way it goes, and I play the game just like everyone else. Why do you think I don't have a car? Didn't you ever wonder about it?" Marty waited for an answer but continued to talk when he didn't get one. "I could run an old jalopy but everyone'd know I couldn't manage something better. This way, I say, 'Me wade through traffic? Not on your life. I take cabs,' and the guys think it's the truth."

Roz stared at him. His reddish-brown hair was brushed back into the suggestion of a pompadour and she thought he looked like a movie star. "Is it so important what the men at your office think?"

"I'm not just another poor slob. They respect me."

The elevated tracks of the Brighton Line were straight ahead and Roz could see a train rounding the curve as they approached the station. She freed her hand from Marty's and turned to look at him.

"This makes no difference to me, but if it matters to you, I know I will be happy there. It is a very beautiful building."

"I guess I'll draw up a budget tonight just to be on the safe side."

The American girls do not worry about money, Roz told herself, and was careful not to let Marty see she feared the other building tenants.

Today, however, Roz determined to become acquainted with some of her new neighbors and tried to figure out the best way while she polished the mirror of her new double dresser. She suppressed an uneasy feeling when the mirror was entirely covered with wax. In Jewish homes, mirrors were covered when someone died. But she felt foolish. There was nothing to worry about and no reason to be afraid of her new neighbors. Surely, she had only to enter that lovely gold and white playground and begin a conversation. Perhaps Cousin Bertha's daughter, Marion, would be there and would help her.

For a moment, as Roz walked to the bedroom closet for something to wear, she considered waiting a few days but forced herself to begin today. She found it hard to decide whether slacks or a casual dress would be more appropriate, and Roz tried to remember how the few women she'd passed in the lobby of the building dressed. The closet, half empty despite a suitcase full of "trousseau" she had brought to her marriage, didn't help.

Her striped cotton print was wrong, Roz noticed immediately upon approaching the Mediterranean Arms playground. One of the other women wore lemon-colored silk slacks, beautifully tailored, blending perfectly with the gold and white benches of the small playground. Despite a slight chill in the air, another woman had on an apricot-colored dress with thin spaghetti straps,

Although small, the playground sported two sizes of swings, sandboxes, slides, and seesaws. Round gold trashcans dominated the corners. At the entrance, a tall girl, her dark pageboy swinging in the slight breeze, walked towards Roz.

"Mama told me to look for you. I'm Marion Davis."

Roz looked at her cousin and saw an attractive, heart-shaped face with high cheekbones that gave her an exotic look.

Calmly waiting to be introduced, a petite young woman with curls the shade of hair Roz knew people called "dirty blonde," stood next to Marion.

"Does Cousin Natalie still live in Florida?"

"For heaven's sake, Marion, if you have relatives in Florida, why don't you fly out there for a visit?" the girl with Marion said. "You can use a change."

"Why I barely know Roz's family."

"They would be most happy to see you," Roz said.

"If it weren't for Mama, I might do it."

"Cousin Bertha would be welcome at any time."

The other girl groaned and Roz looked at her, waited to be acknowledged, and wondered whether they'd noticed her accent. As a new arrival in the United States, she'd felt overwhelmingly shy because of that accent, but now she managed except when meeting people for the first time. She would've completely suppressed the feeling by now if not for the months of Sue Ellen's ridicule down in Miami Beach.

Sandra Kramer finally introduced herself and smiled at Roz as she apologized for Marion's preoccupation. "Where are you from? I can't quite place your accent."

"Cuba, but my parents were German refugees, and I am told my speech has more of a German than a Spanish sound."

"In any case, it's charming," Sandra said.

Roz quickly examined Sandra's face to see whether the girl mocked her, but she appeared serious.

"Roz's family escaped from Germany just in time," Marion explained. "They were able to emigrate to Cuba before she was born. Mama always says how lucky they were."

"It was not luck exactly."

"Well, I'm a foreigner here myself," Sandra said.

"You are not an American?"

"I'm from upstate New York. To these people," Sandra nodded towards the playground where the women sat on benches, their attention equally divided between knitting and talking until occasionally one rocked the nearest carriage with her foot or called to a toddler in the sandbox, "I could as well be from outer space."

"But if you are an American, you are one of them. You belong."

"If not for my husband, I wouldn't be accepted at all," Sandra said. "A handsome man is an asset around here."

Roz imagined she heard a bitter undertone in the words. Sandra seemed unhappier than her own widowed cousin, but before she could wonder why, Marion took her arm.

"This building is friendlier than most places in Brooklyn. You won't have any problems."

"I don't know about that," Sandra said. "But just to start the ball rolling, I'd like to invite you and your husband for Saturday night. Just a small dinner party. Marion is coming and so is my brother."

"I shall look forward to this," Roz said, hating to have Marty meet such attractive women so soon after their marriage, but trying to hide her insecurity.

"That appeals to me more than the little tête-à-tête you wanted to arrange between your brother and me," Marion said, fingering her bangs.

"And beneath that tough exterior, there's a heart as hard as a diamond," Sandra said. "No, it's as hard as that white stone up there." She gazed at the Mediterranean Arms with an expression Roz couldn't decipher.

"Very funny," Marion said. The two of them drifted away, leaving Roz to wish her cousin had taken time to present her to the other ladies. She now had to enter the playground alone.

On one of the gold and white benches, a young mother rummaged for something in a huge, silver baby carriage. A tiny blonde, she looked like a teenager compared to the stocky woman beside her. Both women had knitting in their laps. Roz took a seat next to them.

"Mine never ate more than half a jar of strained carrots at a time. Never." The stout one motioned towards a little boy in the sandbox.

"Ours eats carrots all right but not desserts. Jerome says I shouldn't even offer him any," the blonde told her.

"You know what they say, no baby with a mother around to stuff food down his throat ever starved."

"But what kind of mother doesn't worry? I can't help it."

A child of five or six detached herself from one of the swings, also painted gold and white, and approached the bench.

"When are you taking me for shoes?"

"Don't bother me, Phyllis. You have enough shoes."

"You said I could have patent leather ones like all my friends."

"We'll see. Now go away and leave me alone. I'm talking."

The blonde rocked the silver carriage rhythmically. "He hardly takes any milk."

"They get worse later on. Take my word."

From where she sat, Roz could see the blue-green water of Sheepshead Bay, dotted with small boats, and she wanted to walk across the street, but the women and their failure to acknowledge her presence held her. All these self-assured Americans made Roz feel drab, and she wondered if Marty were aware of the contrast. She listened to the women, wanting to join the conversation but knowing nothing about babies. On the other hand, their experience might be useful when she had a child of her own.

"There's that snob from the second floor."

"Where?"

"Driving her Cadillac into the garage."

For the first time, Roz noticed the entrance to the building's underground garage, just outside the fence to the right of the playground.

At this point, she decided to speak. "I am Roz Geller. We have just moved here."

"Bobbie Feld," the blonde said.

The heavy woman looked Roz over. "Harriet," she said flatly, without adding her last name. Her bulging eyes made Roz think of an iguana.

"It is a lovely day, is it not?"

"Yeah. Look who just drove in there, Harriet. I didn't know they took garage space."

"So it's another thirty dollars a month; their apartment is one of the cheapest in the building."

Roz tried to talk to them about Sheepshead Bay and the ferry trip to Breezy Point but neither of the girls had ever gone on that excursion, and they seemed more interested in the sweaters taking shape on their plastic needles and their commentary on passers-by.

"You know," Bobbie said. "I think you'll win the pool."

Harriet laughed. "That I could have told you weeks ago."

"Pardon. Is it a swimming pool?"

Harriet looked at her again. "We should let you try it, too. Aren't you in Apartment 5R?"

"Say, she's right across the hall from Sandra and Neil. What a chance for inside information," the blonde said.

Roz guessed that they meant Marion's friend, the one who had just been kind enough to invite her to dinner.

"We have a pool going," Harriet said. "Everyone who bets puts in a dollar and the one who picks the nearest date gets the pot."

"What must I guess?"

"It will be hard for her, Harriet. She's new in the building."

"Listen, it's just guesswork. Anyhow, didn't you see her talking to Marion and Sandra?"

Feeling very stupid, certain they indulged in a form of hazing perpetrated on all new tenants or perhaps only on a refugee like herself, Roz waited.

"Okay, I'll explain," the blonde said. She gave the silver carriage one more decisive rock, adjusted the brake, and leaned back against the bench. "We're betting on how long it takes Marion Davis to steal Sandra Kramer's husband."

Roz stared at the women. I do not believe it, she told herself but the thought of her own husband chilled her. What chance would she have if her exotic cousin wanted him?

"Harriet bet the shortest time in this pool—two months and the way it looks, she may win."

"Of course, I'll win."

"But why Sandra's husband?" Roz asked. "If what you say is true, it could be any man."

"You don't have to worry." Harriet glanced pointedly at Roz' dress. "Marion is out for the big fish."

Roz bit the cuticle of her thumb. "She is my cousin; that is, her mother is the cousin of my mother. They call each other Cousin Natalie and Cousin Bertha. We are relatives."

"I didn't know that," the blonde said.

"Talk about inside information, this is the girl who'll know it first."

"Cut it out, Harriet."

"My cousin Bertha, who is Marion's mother has done much for my family. We owe her our lives."

"All right, don't get excited. You can't blame Marion. Neil's a real dreamboat," Bobbie said.

"A dreamboat with money."

"I do not know my cousin well, but she certainly would not do this. What I have heard—in the family you understand—is that she is very sad, very lonely since her husband died."

"Sure. And she spends her evenings with Sandra and Neil."

Roz looked up the street in the direction Marion had gone and wondered again if it could be true. I will see for myself, she thought, when we have dinner with all of them Saturday night.

"If I win," Harriet said, "I'll buy a beaded evening blouse."

"I have just remembered. Yes, yes, I knew it could not be true."

"Why not?"

"We are all having dinner together Saturday night and Sandra said something about a brother. Surely her brother is the escort, the date, for Marion."

"You are naive," Harriet said.

Bobbie resumed her knitting; the needles clicked almost in time to her words. "That's one way for Sandra to handle the situation."

"Keep your eyes open, kid, and you'll discover why Sandra is so anxious to steer her best friend and her brother together."

Roz started to work another piece of cuticle off her finger, but controlled herself. One must have loyalty to a cousin; it was her responsibility to change the subject.

"Can we not walk along Sheepshead Bay and watch the fishermen? It is very inviting."

"My God, that's for tourists."

"The benches aren't even clean on that side of the street," Bobbie said, patting the gold and white finish of the one she occupied.

Glancing at the tree-shaded walks along the Bay, Roz was tempted to get up and cross the street alone, but she and Marty had signed a three-year lease on their apartment and these women would be her neighbors for a long time.

"Get a load of that; she dyed her hair." Harriet peered at a car that had just approached the ramp to the garage.

"Didn't you know? I heard it yesterday," Bobbie said and turned to Roz. "This is a very interesting place."

Roz heard her words through a pang of despair as she wondered if she would spend the rest of her life this way.

Fotolia #24246474 - Brooklyn Bridge, New York City, USA © BigDog

If she hadn't been dazzled by Neil and could relive the night she'd met Eddie, Marion wondered now, would her life have been guilt free and happy?

Chapter 4

S andra and Neil Kramer's apartment was located in the same line as Marion's, two floors higher. Kitchen, gallery, doorways and closets were exactly where Marion expected them to be, but it always shocked her to see the ebony finishes and deep reds and oranges of her friend's furniture—so different from her own traditional style.

Sandra was nowhere in sight when Marion arrived, but Neil Kramer, tall and rugged in an open-necked blue sport shirt and khaki slacks, took Marion's arm and moved her smoothly across the apartment to the large gray sofa. A muffled greeting came from Sandra in the kitchen, causing Marion to resist Neil's pressure on her arm. "I should help."

"Sandra can manage perfectly."

Neil raised his voice. "Isn't that right, honey?" Without waiting for a reply he settled Marion on the sofa.

"I'll make it up to Sandra another time," Marion said.

"You seem tired tonight, anyhow."

Marion rubbed the dark shadows under her eyes and wished her fingers could make them disappear.

"Don't do that!" Neil pulled her hands away from her face. "Those shadows make you look sort of worldly and experienced."

"Old."

"Come off it. You're lovely. I like thin girls who still have great curves."

"It's been a long time between compliments for me."

"You need a man around to admire you every day." Neil fingered a fold of Marion's flare skirt. "What is this material?"

"Silk."

"That shows how much I know about the ladies' garment industry." Neil's dark eyebrows thickened together when he laughed. He continued to touch the dress softly.

"You make me feel desirable again." She wanted to ruffle his smooth dark hair, feel the pomade she guessed he used. Whatever it was, it had a wonderful, spicy scent.

"You'll dazzle my brother-in-law, Marion."

So Neil helped Sandra with her matchmaking plans. Marion turned away from him.

"We haven't seen much of you lately," he said.

"It's different now."

"Not that much different."

In answer, Marion moved her hand with a helpless gesture and Neil caught hold of it.

"You know I would do anything to help."

"You have helped. Both of you." If Sandra's brother arrived now, he would see her from the doorway of the apartment, and his first view would be of a girl on the sofa holding hands with Neil. She wondered if he were at all like Neil.

"Don't let Sandra talk you into anything."

"Tell me what's wrong with her brother."

"Nothing; he's a great guy, but you need someone special. Someone who can take you to romantic places like Cartagena or Rio the way I can."

Neil's voice had been low but Sandra hurried into the living room. "Are you running Eddie down again?"

"Marion can draw her own conclusions."

"See that you don't criticize Eddie," Sandra said sharply.

Marion blamed herself for the situation, the only discord she'd ever witnessed between Sandra and Neil. "You didn't tell me what he looks like," she said.

"When you're in school, you worry whether a blind date is tall, dark and handsome or fits your preconceived idea of looks, but you should have developed less shallow criteria by now."

"I wonder what happened to our new neighbors," Neil said, coming to Marion's rescue.

"Wouldn't you guess she's too timid to arrive early?"

Not like me, Marion thought. The first to get here, anxious and old-maidish. "Why did you invite them?"

"Roz is a nice kid. The husband really cares for her, too. I could tell that the day we saw them together in the elevator."

"I hope she doesn't mention Eddie to Mama."

"Come on, Marion. She's a newlywed and you're definitely not the center of her universe."

Marion found it hard to identify that caustic voice with Sandra. She might be harried with preparations for dinner, but that seemed unlikely. The set table and the aroma from the kitchen showed that all went well there. Toby was probably still awake, waiting for his chance to march out of bed, but that was nothing new.

"I'll tell you why I invited them," Sandra said. "I'm sorry for that girl. She'll have trouble with the ladies of the Mediterranean Arms, and I thought she needed one or two friends in the building."

The doorbell called Sandra across the apartment. From where she sat on the sofa in full view of the doorway, Marion tried to appear uninterested in the new arrival.

"Always late," Sandra said as she brought him over to meet Marion, who eyed him curiously. Why doesn't he get contact lenses, she wondered, noticing the heavy brown frames of his glasses. Eddie, slightly built like his sister with the same blue eyes and the same curly blond hair, had an intense expression.

"And my students really appreciate it. When an instructor doesn't show, they can escape after a ten minute wait."

"You ought to break that late habit," Sandra said.

Marion noticed Eddie's flicker of surprise at his sister's acerbity. If he guessed it stemmed from Sandra's anxiety for him to make a good impression on her friend, he gave no indication, but for Marion this seemed a sign that matchmaking had begun and would never stop until she succumbed.

"I usually meet them in the corridor," Eddie said. "After a few groans, they turn around and go back to class."

A childish groan that sounded like an attempt to mimic Eddie sounded behind him. He turned and scooped up Toby. "Why aren't you in bed, young man?"

"You have to call me Chief Thundercloud."

"Isn't it past your bedtime, Chief?"

"Put me down, you."

"Please put me down, you."

"Let him down, Eddie. I'll take him back to his bed," Sandra said.

"Oh, let him stay up for a while," Neil told her. "Toby wants to see everyone."

"Will you behave?" Sandra asked, caressing his silky blond curls. "You always spoil him," she told Neil.

Toby scrambled onto the couch next to Marion. "I get to stay up with the company."

"That's nice," Marion said.

Eddie laughed. "Even a four-year-old knows how seriously to take that remark." He sat down on the other side of Toby. "Do you live in a wigwam or a tepee?"

"A wigwam."

"What do you suppose Indians used for light in their wigwams, Chief?"

Toby pointed to one of the lamps.

"They didn't have lamps. Indians went to sleep when it got dark and woke up as soon as the sun came out in the morning."

"Goodnight, Uncle Eddie." As the adults watched, Toby hopped out of the living room, trying to imitate an Indian dancer. Their laughter still rang out when the bell sounded Roz and Marty's arrival.

"The Gellers live right across the hall in apartment 5R," Sandra told Eddie as she introduced them.

"How did 5R get opposite 5G?"

"Listen to the upstate hick!" Neil said.

"Ah, my husband, the native-born New Yorker. Brooklyn, if you please, not upstate like us hicks."

What's wrong with Sandra tonight, Marion wondered, thankful that the newcomers seemed unaware of her friend's mood.

Roz, awkward-looking in a yellow print of some rayon blend, remained glued to her husband's side while he appeared to size up the apartment. To Marion, Marty Geller seemed a know-it-all with the type of physique girls called "shlubby" in her dating years.

The brief recollection of her dating days chilled Marion. My life is moving backwards, she thought. Perhaps Eddie's more promising than one like Marty Geller who will never amount to anything, but I don't want to play the dating game again.

Neil had taken over the conversation. "My partner leaves for Cartagena tomorrow."

"No kidding," Marty said.

"We've got to visit our coffee accounts every year, spread a little goodwill."

Marion recognized Neil's longing. "When do you get to travel?"

"Anytime I want. Right now, I let Sidney make the business trips because Toby's so young."

A good friend would offer to keep Toby for them, Marion told herself. But what would she do with him? She didn't know the first thing about children.

"When I take over the outside work, our imports will double," Neil said. "Down at the office today, I had to set everything up for Sidney. That clown doesn't know which end is up."

"Buy him out," Eddie suggested.

Neil glared at his brother-in-law and went on to explain all the details involved in a goodwill tour of coffee plantations.

"When Neil and I go to South America for the firm," Sandra said, "we'll live it up. All the coffee people will entertain us and afterwards we'll see other countries on our own."

"I'd love to travel," Marion said. She was determined not to envy Sandra, but couldn't help seeing herself in Rio de Janeiro with Neil.

"In my company, I don't have a chance in hell for that kind of assignment," Marty said.

"Eddie's going to Spain," his sister told them.

"You lucky son-of-a-gun," Marty told him.

"My sister's an optimist. Actually, my grant hasn't come through for the research I want to do in early Spanish drama. I don't think I can manage a year in Spain without it."

"Why don't you get some commission work?" Marty asked. "Don't tell me you've never seen advertisements in the Times offering commissions all over the world."

"Surely, it's not that easy."

"That's a racket," Neil said. "Don't fall for it."

"Hell, no," Marty said. "My company just paid a fellow going to Germany on his own business."

"What do I know about business? I'm a teacher." Eddie shifted around to look at Neil. "After all, as my brother-in-law has often pointed out, I've never met a payroll."

"I can tell you've got an outgoing personality. It'd be a cinch for you. The company tells the guy exactly who to see and what to say."

"Well, it's a thought," Eddie said.

"Try it, Eddie. One of us has to have a chance," Sandra said. To Marion, she sounded close to hysteria and now she guessed her friend's mood stemmed from disappointment.

Here was Neil's partner, a man who obviously wasn't anywhere as good as Neil, making an exciting trip while Sandra and Neil were stuck at home with their child. I'll try to be friendly to Eddie, Marion thought. At least she won't have to worry about that.

"Dinner's ready," Sandra said.

The dining table had been extended to seat six, but evidently unconcerned with formal seating arrangements, Sandra had placed everyone where she felt it would do the most good. Marion found herself sitting next to Eddie along one end of the table, opposite Roz and Marty.

"Wait a minute, I'll help," Neil said and disappeared into the kitchen with Sandra.

Now it will be all right, Marion thought as they carried out the appetizer and both joined the others at the table.

"Take note," Eddie said to Marion. "When bachelor brother dines with married sister, menu consists of his favorite foods."

"But will your favorites be mine?"

"That's anybody's guess."

Marion smiled and pushed aside the parsley garnishing her plate of chopped liver. She didn't really care whether Eddie liked her, so she could relax. Obviously, Sandra had the good looks in the family, although her brother was not unattractive in his earnestness. She could picture Neil's ruggedly handsome face without turning toward him for comparison. Sandra had the better deal.

"My sister said that you're a Hunter College grad. Did you take any Spanish literature courses?"

"My language was German."

"Ach so! With ex-Spanish students, I slip into the romance of the Golden Age, but we'll have to begin at the beginning, lamb."

Probably one of a dozen different lines, Marion decided, but she was flattered by the intellectual approach, and she'd promised herself to be nice to him. "Tell me about the Golden Age."

"Few people know even the major Spanish writers," Eddie said and he was off.

"It is not easy," Marion heard Roz say. "So many times I am made to remember I am a foreigner." She must be talking to Neil.

"Don't worry about it," Sandra said, leaning over Roz as she scooped up the used dishes. "This should be the happiest time of your life, so enjoy it while it lasts."

"Neil is a wonderful husband," Marion said to Eddie, as she watched Neil excuse himself to help his wife.

"Is that what women want? Wouldn't it be less complicated to hire a part-time maid?"

The soup, in line with Sandra's helter-skelter way of mixing Jewish recipes with French or Chinese or Italian dishes, was minestrone. Eddie ate slowly, glancing at Marion from time to time.

"There's an off-Broadway production of "La vida es sueño," by Calderón. Will you come with me?"

"I don't understand Spanish."

"On alternate nights, they do the play in English."

"But I don't know the play."

"It's a masterpiece. Even my students enjoy it."

"I don't think I can..."

"What a wonderful experience for you. Almost like being introduced to Shakespeare for the first time." Eddie slouched in his chair and smiled up at Marion. "A week from tonight?"

Something tactful. Another appointment. Marion looked around the table, trying to find a way out.

"You look trapped. Did my little brother-in-law propose or proposition?"

Neil had been listening and now probably the rest of them as well. Searching for something light to say, Marion could only recall Aunt Lena's words about having someone to sleep with again. Her glance moved to Neil and back to Eddie. Why was he so insistent when there were a million pretty girls to date?

"You live in this building, don't you? I'll call for you at seven o'clock next Saturday."

"Take my car," Neil offered. "We won't need it that night."

Why was Neil forcing her into a decision? He didn't even like his brother-in-law.

"He is very fine," Roz whispered as she put down one of the individual veal casseroles she helped Sandra serve.

"It's too soon." It was impossible to start from the beginning again. Marion wanted to shout at them to leave her alone.

"Why are you afraid?" Eddie asked softly.

I must not try for the life I want and fail again, she answered silently. "I haven't been going out."

"You have to start eventually." She noticed a boyish crease in his chin when he smiled at her.

"I guess I do need to break out." But God knows, he's not a bit like Alec, Marion told herself.

Marion remembered how important Saturday night dates had once been for her. She would carefully tweeze her eyebrows in the morning, set off for the hairdresser, and then wait impatiently for evening while she dressed and made up long before her date's arrival. She'd kept to the same schedule with Eddie, even though she'd convinced herself the excitement was missing.

Chapter 5

Maybe Eddie will take me to a party after the theatre, Marion daydreamed. Aunt Lena used to claim that one boyfriend led to another. At the party she would meet someone taller and better looking than Eddie. An artist. No, not another artist. What about an older man in the foreign service? Nothing cloak and daggerish, exactly... Marion laughed at her fantasy. But these things do happen, she thought, studying herself in the mirror. She felt glamorous enough to meet anyone tonight even though her dark hair was uncomfortably stiff. No point visiting Mama with newly styled hair and blonde highlights when she wanted to avoid questions about her date, so she'd saved the hairdresser until late that afternoon. In the old days, Aunt Lena mourned when Marion had no Saturday night date, but Mama always looked relieved. Well, neither of them would know about Eddie.

Marion smoothed iridescent taupe eye shadow over her lids and wondered what sort of evening she could expect. If Eddie were special, she reasoned, someone would have snatched him long ago. At best, he represented a few hours respite from loneliness. But this, Marion's first date since Alec's death, had to be a turning point. All at once, excitement did take hold and she looked forward to Eddie's arrival.

Perhaps it was the gray topcoat over a charcoal suit, but when Eddie appeared, he seemed more presentable than he had before.

"Please sit down. That sofa is more comfortable than it looks."

"So am I."

Although the days were warm, evenings could cool down; Marion decided to wear a lightweight coat, too. She noticed Eddie turning over ashtrays and figurines one by one to read the marks.

"I see that you collect antiques," he said.

"It's fun pretending that the plate over there or that cigarette box you just looked at once belonged to royalty."

"You do have one or two good pieces. I like your style."

"Are you a collector, too?"

"Rather a pretentious claim for me. I do intend to make a real hobby of it someday, though."

"A neighbor of mine on the second floor bought the most exquisite desk," Marion said. "A sort of greenish color that goes perfectly with her green carpets. Then she recovered her couch in a green and blue print. It's just gorgeous."

"Do you care so much for things like that?"

"Well, I wouldn't consider doing mine over right now, but I get ideas when I'm invited into other apartments in the Arms."

"We'll have to antique together one of these days."

"You're not like the teachers I had in college," Marion told him.

"In class, I scowl."

"Then I'm glad I wasn't in your classes." Marion heard herself echo early party and dance conversations. If only they could skip the opening moves of the game, she thought and found Eddie had anticipated her.

"Let's forget about trivia tonight, Marion. There are enough real conversational possibilities."

"I know. The newspapers are full of them."

"There's that. For someone who's been married, boy meets girl talk must be very dull."

Marion kept silent all the way down to the lobby, wondering what to say to him now. As they walked the short block to the parked car he'd borrowed from Neil, she tried several beginnings, but they all seemed inadequate. Eddie suggested avoiding chitchat, she thought. Let him take the lead.

He held the car door open for Marion; the gesture reminded her he was an out-of-towner, with a background different from the Brooklyn boys she'd once dated. By the time they'd started up Ocean Avenue, somehow Marion had told him more about Alec than she'd ever told his sister.

"You come so close emotionally and physically, learn so much about the other person. I know Alec would have been a great artist and now all his talent has been unrealized."

"Don't you have his canvases?"

"I wish I'd shown them to you. Some are unfinished. They depress me more than the others."

"Have you tried to exhibit them, enter them in art shows?"

"I've been afraid."

"Of what? That they'll say he wasn't any good after all, that you'll lose faith in him?"

Marion had never put her fear into words. "Maybe later on, when I'm less emotional about Alec's death. Sometimes I feel almost as if he'd deliberately abandoned me."

"Genuine rejection is different."

"It's silly of me," Marion said. "But I seem to have so little control over my imagination now."

"A man who's been rejected suffers more than a girl in the same situation. The girl can always claim it happened because she wouldn't sleep with him or because she did sleep with him, while the man has no excuses to give his friends or himself. She didn't want him, period. It takes a long time for the ego to absorb that blow."

How could anyone compare being jilted to being widowed? To Marion, Eddie sounded like a perpetual schlemiel, who wanted only the girls he couldn't have. Before the end of the evening, he would make a pass; leading up to it by way of conversational intimacy.

Eddie waited for the light to change and looked at her intently until the first horn blasts began behind him. "In your case, it's harder to come to terms with the finality of being left alone by Alec because you believe your mother caused it."

Marion placed her hands carefully into the pockets of her coat to hide their trembles. "I don't blame Mama," she insisted. "You got that idea from your sister."

"Sandra's an extremely perceptive person."

The drive into Manhattan in the heavy Saturday night traffic was stop-and-go all along. At the next red light, Eddie turned toward her again. "You're very lovely, Marion."

She murmured a polite reply.

"But why let them put those blonde highlights or whatever they're called on your hair? You don't need it."

She tried to hide her fury. This routine also had been part of adolescent dating, insults traded to gain some self-assurance. "Perhaps that's a matter of taste."

"Agreed. But without the blonde streak, you would look so much more natural."

"Are you trying to change me on our first date?"

"That's usually considered the woman's prerogative, isn't it?"

Apparently his good humor could withstand her anger. "I wouldn't dare suggest that your tie is the wrong shade for that gray suit."

"You don't like to hear the truth, do you?"

They had reached the theatre and Eddie dropped Marion off to wait in the lobby while he parked the car. Other women whose escorts were engaged in the parking battle, overflowed the lobby. By the time Eddie returned, Marion, diverted by the show of new styles, had forgotten their discussion.

"Look at that stunning dress!"

Eddie didn't turn but assumed what she guessed to be his classroom voice and lectured her on "La vida es sueño" until the play began. Marion didn't mind listening to him. Other than using his knowledge of Spanish literature to impress her, Eddie had nothing. He didn't even have a car of his own.

While on stage Segismundo railed against his miserable life, Marion leaned over to whisper to Eddie, "You didn't tell me it would be so old-fashioned."

"Be quiet and listen! It's beautiful."

During the intermission, Eddie quoted to her from the original Spanish:

"¿Habra otro," entre sí decía,
"más pobre y triste que yo?"
Y cuando el rostro volvía,
Halló la respuesta, viendo
que iba otro sabio cogiendo
las hojas que él arrojó.

"Was that when Rosaura told about the other sage, who picked up the leaves the first one threw away?" Marion asked. "Straight Pollyanna."

"It's true, though."

"God knows, it doesn't make me any less unhappy to know that someone else is more miserable."

"You think about it. Calderón has more to offer than most of the junk you're accustomed to see and read. This play will be around when we're both dead."

"Just because it's old."

He smiled at her, an odd smile that made his expression gentle despite his willingness to argue the point. "You sound like my students. 'Just because it's old, what makes it good, Mr. Berg?' What can I tell them? The writers and artists I admire most have all been dead for hundreds of years. They became known and endured without phony hype or advertising."

"I don't know much about "La vida es sueño," but I don't agree with you. Alec used to say paintings were merely photographs until the invention of the camera. Without modern art, paintings would be boring."

"What did Alec paint?"

"Landscapes, mostly."

"Well, then?"

"They weren't photographs. He painted them as seen through a mist, sort of hazy." Since Alec's death, Marion often saw things that way herself, especially the hallways of the Mediterranean Arms where she found herself wandering in dreams. Sometimes, it also happened when she left the apartment alone or stepped out of the elevator by herself.

Intermission over, Eddie seemed absorbed by the play, but the action caught Marion only a few times. Medieval church questions of free will were difficult to follow and she switched her mind to debate whether she wanted to see Eddie again. She decided that he had very little imagination, which he proved by taking her to Howard Johnson's after the play.

"You would have preferred a musical comedy," he said as they waited for a table.

"No, something different. Experimental."

"Thought-provoking."

"That's right."

"Then you missed the point of "La vida es sueño," Eddie said. "It's all about illusion and reality. Should have been good for you."

"What do you mean by that?"

"Among other things you should be aware it's an illusion that the dead were perfect."

"Alec was exceptional." She bit her lip to control her anger.

"Since I never knew him, I'll have to grant that point. But surely you can transfer all that hero worship to a living man now."

"How many exciting men are there? Your sister has one; I had one. But there are very few men who can offer a glamorous life, not mere existence."

"Something glossy like a magazine advertisement."

"Don't make fun of me. I know people do have the life I want."

"Marion, a bright girl can figure out many things, if she wants to figure them out. Think of the characters in the play tonight. Like them, you'll either awaken to the truth or ultimately fall."

She shivered and glanced quickly around the restaurant for reassurance. The well-dressed couples gave her confidence in her own future. "Look at that kooky hairdo, Eddie. I'm dying."

"Why do you deliberately make yourself sound shallow?"

"Do you feel superior when you criticize me?"

When he winced, Marion knew her words had hit the mark.

"A lovely young widow like you—I'd pictured you ennobled by suffering, not taking refuge in the superficial." Eddie slouched down in his seat and lowered his voice. "If I didn't like you, I wouldn't bother with frankness."

Suddenly Marion saw herself on an endless procession of such dates with friends and brothers of people she knew. I won't do it; I have to control my own destiny.

"And don't retreat into hurt silence," Eddie added, but she remained quiet until they started back to Brooklyn. Traffic had dwindled now and Marion calculated she'd be rid of Eddie within three-quarters of an hour.

"I'm just a poor boy from Syracuse, but I'm not impressed by the big city."

Among Marion's neighbors and friends, probably all would forego food rather than admit they couldn't afford something. To state you were poor was unbelievable.

"I'm sick and tired of the phoniness. You girls didn't get through college on charm alone. Surely there's something behind the bleached heads."

She'd have to laugh it off or they would have a terrible argument. "And what are the girls like in Syracuse?"

"When I first arrived here, the glamor impressed me. Oh God, was I impressed! I tried very hard to keep you sophisticated New Yorkers from finding out what a hick I was."

"But the girl who threw you over—wasn't she also from upstate?" Why did I say something so tactless, Marion reproached herself.

"You're not at all like her," Eddie suddenly said.

In front of them, a car made a left turn without signaling, and the brakes squealed as Eddie stopped short. He shook his fist at the other driver. "That's what I learned in this city."

Marion was afraid when she noticed how tightly he gripped the steering wheel. "As soon as I ask the frank questions, you change the subject."

"You want to know? All right, I'll tell you. Pauline and I were in high school together. The only one I could ever talk to, the one I wanted to spend my life with, which probably sounds corny to you."

"Maybe it was only because you were both very young." Marion said and added, "Is she married?"

"I'd never have left Syracuse otherwise."

"You say that now, but you would have left to teach here in any case."

"Call me a fool," Eddie said, "but I'd rather have taught at the high school level back home while there was any possibility of Pauline changing her mind."

They approached Sheepshead Bay and Eddie took the first empty parking space. She agreed when he suggested they stroll alongside the Bay for a few blocks, but her heels were too high for comfort and, after a time, she asked him to turn back.

"We probably do see ourselves perpetually as eighteen-year olds," Eddie said. "Girls and boys."

"You're wrong. I could barely wait to grow up."

"Our adolescent attitudes towards life and love stay with us forever."

"If my husband..."

"Forget the rose-colored way you remember your marriage."

"We loved each other. I don't have to prove it to you."

"I don't want to hurt you, lamb, but your marriage was adolescent, too. Based on hero worship. I told you that before."

"And you're an adult," Marion flared.

"I'm just beginning to understand that Pauline and I had a similar relationship to the one between you and Alec. I see that now, but you still refuse to face the truth."

Marion waited for him to go on, looked at the slight figure and wished for some magnetism, that she could be attracted to him physically. An easy solution to all her problems.

"I like walking with you." After a moment, he took a deep breath of the salty air and she found herself copying him. The air near the ocean did seem fresher than in the rest of the city, but Marion had never concerned herself with that phenomenon. If you wanted to be a New Yorker, the fumes went with the city in the same way noise, traffic, and crowds did. Others in the building talked of moving to California or Florida but Marion had never been tempted to leave Brooklyn permanently.

She wanted jet-set glamour, the ability to hop a plane to Europe or South America while keeping New York as home base. When she watched the colorful sailboats in Sheepshead Bay, she wished someone would come to take her away in one of them.

Eddie seemed reluctant to cross the street to the Mediterranean Arms. Now, they stood at the edge of the Bay, while occasional late traffic turned into West End Avenue.

"Are you too conventional to ask me in for a cup of coffee?"

"Do I seem so unsophisticated?"

"It's hard to explain just how you affect me. It's eluded me all evening."

"Actually the doorman on duty will notice. I mean, if you don't come right down again after taking me to my apartment, he might gossip."

Eddie smiled at her. "Not a bad excuse."

"No, really. My neighbors don't gossip, but the people who work here might."

"Since you live in a building with twenty-four hour doorman service, you should learn to ignore that."

"I can't. What people think about me is important to me."

"So I see," Eddie said drily. "All right. We'll talk now. I'd like to take you for a drive next week on the Island or to Connecticut. Antique hunting."

"I'm not sure."

"Not sure you're free or not sure you want to see me again?"

He seemed so vulnerable. "It sounds like fun," Marion said instead of the flat refusal she had ready.

"As soon as I know when Neil will let me have his car, I'll call you."

"Wouldn't a car of your own be more convenient?" There, she could be tactful. Perhaps his car was in for service or repair. Or he could be one of those people who bragged about the difficulties of keeping a car in New York and finally gave it up to emphasize the point.

"Can't afford one."

Marion, who'd never heard a date declare outright that he couldn't afford something, looked at Eddie in surprise.

"If I'm ever to get to Spain, the nonessentials can't fetter me." He sounded pleased with himself, his manner unapologetic.

"Well, if you can use Neil's whenever you need it ..."

"Only for you. I rarely bother Sandra and Neil."

Now that she'd agreed to see him either Saturday or Sunday of the following week, Eddie was ready to leave Sheepshead Bay. He took her hand and they crossed the street to the Mediterranean Arms, where the doorman, having spotted them as they walked toward the building entrance, held open the outer door. This time, Marion thought as she entered the cool lobby, she would not be alone in the elevator nor down through the long corridors. For the moment, she was Segismundo in his palace, not in his prison tower.

Fotolia #32107417 - Grand Army Plaza in Prospect Park, Brooklyn © SeanPavonePhoto

Marion thought back over the years to the time when her cousin, Roz Geller had become her closest (and sometimes only) friend .It hadn't started that way. At first, she was too self-absorbed to pay much attention to her cousin, but later they'd often talked about Roz's own experiences in the Mediterranean Arms.

Chapter 6

W hen Roz Geller first heard about the series of burglaries in the Mediterranean Arms, she regretted moving into the building, but couldn't convince Marty. The Arms was the only place to live; everyone in Brooklyn knew the building, he told Roz. The white stone façade and the gold and white playground were noticeable despite the profusion of new apartment houses. If necessary, Marty would moonlight, using the income from an extra job solely for the apartment. He was ready to make any sacrifice to keep the Arms as his address.

"I won't move unless we can go into something bigger and better," he told Roz.

"Can we someday buy a home of our own?"

"A private house? Sure, we'll end off on the Island with the rest of the young families."

"But Marty, meanwhile, I am afraid of being robbed."

"Why should we worry? Let the big shots shiver over their wives' jewels and furs. Better yet, let them take a safe deposit box instead of showing off, and there wouldn't be any break-ins."

"But whoever it is doesn't know we're poor."

"Sh-h." Marty looked around as though he could be overheard. "I don't want to hear that word. We're not rich, but we're sure as hell not poor."

"But…"

"These guys are smart, Roz. They don't crack an apartment blindly." He closed the venetian blinds and turned on the one living room lamp, a hand-me-down from his parents. "We won't be robbed and neither will your friends across the hall."

"But the Kramers are rich."

"Don't make me laugh. He's just a four flusher."

"The ladies in the playground say…"

"Don't tell me. I grew up in a building like this. Okay, so the rent was forty-six bucks instead of a hundred and ninety-four a month, but the yentas were the same."

"I like Sandra," Roz ventured timidly, trying to be honest.

"Sandra's a good kid."

"She is nicer to me than the other ladies. Even better than the daughter of Cousin Bertha."

"Now there's one who's asking for it. If I were in the business, Marion Davis is the first one I'd rob."

"The way you speak, it is as if you want that to happen."

"I got nothing against her."

Roz covered her cheeks with her hands to cool them and couldn't avoid a small moan. Whenever she heard Marion's name mentioned, she remembered what the neighbors were betting on.

"If your cousin keeps making eyes at Neil Kramer, she'll get more than she deserves."

Since Roz had never told her husband about the pool, she decided he must have heard of it elsewhere. "But Marty, you know she is dating the brother of Sandra."

"There's a nice guy, but he's not going to make out."

"The brother has such a sad face, almost as if he is also a refugee."

"Yeah, a refugee from Syracuse. Now don't you get soft on him."

"Marty!"

"He's only a teacher, anyhow. Probably makes less than I do."

"What a man earns is not important."

"It is in Brooklyn, kid. It's the whole story."

From the street, five flights below came a bellow, "Back up a little more, bud, and you'll lose a fender."

"Everyone has the angry face and the angry voice here," Roz said. "Why, when they have so much?"

"I don't know."

"But what makes them so unhappy?"

"You don't believe it now, but one of these days, we'll probably have the same dissatisfied looks as the rest of them." He turned on the television and stopped talking.

The next afternoon, Roz, though not convinced, dressed in new aqua silk slacks she'd bought on sale and went downstairs to discover whether her neighbors also worried about the danger of break-ins.

The playground was empty except for Harriet and her little boy but by now Roz knew the others would gradually straggle downstairs as the day advanced. Harriet, her puffiness accentuated by pink pedal pushers, read a Dr. Seuss book to her toddler while he pounded on the book and yelled "no, no, no" at intervals. Remaining just inside the gate to the playground, Roz waited for Harriet to notice her.

"Grab a seat. You're out early. Boy, if this little pest didn't drive me crazy, I wouldn't show my face before lunch."

"But it is so nice in the morning."

"Take my word, it's no fun waiting for the elevator, rushing down like this and back upstairs for lunch and down again after lunch and up again if I forget something or if the little pest starts nagging for a cookie."

"Cookie, cookie," the little boy started yelling.

"Shut up or I'll slam you." Harriet turned to Roz. "Then at three o'clock, Phyllis comes home from school and my troubles really begin. If you're smart, you'll wait a few years before you have children."

Roz felt herself blush. She knew the women here made no secret of these details, but she didn't want Harriet to learn that she had no intention of waiting.

"By the way, how's your cousin's romance?"

"There is no such thing. Marion dates the brother of Sandra."

"That's a good one. I can tell you just how that affair will turn out." From somewhere in her knitting bag, Harriet withdrew a small pail and shovel for the little boy and pushed him over to the sandbox. "How's it going with you newlyweds?"

"Okay." Roz didn't want to be rude but she couldn't accept personal questions casually.

"How about that—a happy marriage in this building!"

"Surely most are happy, especially all the good-looking young couples here. They have so much; they are so carefree."

"I could tell you a few things," Harriet said. "There's a couple on the second floor getting an annulment and they just got married in February."

"But Jewish people would not ..."

"That's what you think. Another girl in 6N, from a good Jewish home, is drinking herself into a sanatorium, and the night doorman told me that 1G has a man who sleeps over whenever her husband's out of town."

"Perhaps he is a relative."

As though imploring someone to witness Roz's innocence, Harriet looked around the playground. "Relative, my eye. Relatives don't sneak out at four in the morning. The ones who keep telling you how much their husbands love them and what wonderful presents they get are the worst."

"It is cruel to have everybody take notice."

"When they carry on that way?"

"Perhaps there is a reason."

Harriet snorted. "My husband wouldn't look at another woman."

If only I could be as self-assured as this American woman, Roz thought, and remembered what she had come down to find out. "I have wanted to ask you, are the other ladies worried about burglaries?"

"You have to expect break-ins if you want to live in a high-class place. Naturally, they'd rather do a job here than in Bensonhurst."

"But you are not afraid?"

"Why should I worry? We're insured."

"Well, hi!" The slim blonde, Roberta, walked past their bench conspicuously carrying a Saks Fifth Avenue box.

"Where've you been, Bobbie?" Harriet called out in her shrill voice.

"Shopping the whole morning. My mother-in-law took the baby."

"Lucky you."

"He is such a sweet baby, you must already miss him," Roz said.

"I'm going to sleep all afternoon, as a matter of fact."

"But are they not easy to care for when they are so little?"

"When I feed that baby, I sometimes think it will never end, that I'll spend my life holding his bottle."

"Just leave the television set on and sit in front of it while you feed him."

Roz looked quickly at Harriet to see whether she was joking.

"Except that Jerome would kill me, I'd prop the bottle and not go near the crib until burping time."

"Here's what you do," Harriet said. "Put him on his tummy with his head turned to one side and the bottle in his mouth and stuff a few folded diapers under the bottle. Jerome will never know the difference if you don't have a bottle holder in the house."

"He sure can't ask the baby," Roberta said and hurried towards the lobby entrance.

It is a long way from breastfeeding, Roz thought and wondered if that was why the women all had time to dress themselves and their children so beautifully. Of course, there seemed to be two distinct groups in the building, as she'd noticed before from talk in the little park. Some women bragged about natural childbirth and breastfeeding while others seemed to glory in how much anesthesia they'd had and how little they did personally for the baby.

The latter group had monogrammed diapers, formula service, and cleaning girls, but they seemed to have money enough for it all. Roz wondered if she would ever belong in this building.

"I'd like to go upstairs, too, but my girl is cleaning. If I let him run around," Harriet nodded towards the little boy in the sandbox, "while Mary works, next week will find me training a new girl."

"Are they expensive?"

A malicious grin spread over Harriet's chubby face. "You remind me of the man buying a Rolls Royce who asked how many miles he'd get to the gallon of gas. Listen, if you live in a classy place, you can't worry about the upkeep."

Roz looked across at the bluish green water of Sheepshead Bay and searched for an answer to the question in the other woman's eyes. What was she doing here? She could reply, "My husband wished us to begin marriage with everything our own parents never had." Roz hoped it was the real reason because if she went over it too often in her mind, she suspected Marty wanted only to make an impression on complete strangers.

"You know, they're very particular here," Harriet said. "Mr. Fontanna doesn't just let anyone in, and he can throw out a tenant who lowers the tone of the building."

"Throw out?"

"Sure. The lease has an eviction clause, in case you didn't see it, I can tell you it's a tough one."

"But if you pay the rent on time..."

"That doesn't mean anything. Today everyone has money to burn."

Marion and Sandra strolled past the playground carrying packages and Roz, who realized her neighbor enjoyed her discomfort, took the initiative and called to them.

"I must sit down for a minute, I'm beat," Sandra said.

Marion followed her through the gate and they sat under one of the gold and white sun umbrellas.

"That is a lot to carry," Roz said, thinking how attractive her cousin looked even with her hair hidden under a paisley scarf. Not many women could carry that off.

"You should see what's coming with United Parcel," Marion told her. "I bought the most beautiful bathing suit with a matching beachrobe so I can dream about vacationing in Bermuda or another exotic beach resort."

"Among other things," Sandra said and smiled at her friend. "It's early to bed for me tonight and next time I shop with you, remind me to take vitamins first. I'm just a country girl mangled by big city crowds."

"Go on, you love the city the same as I do."

"For an out-of-towner, you certainly managed to grab a dreamboat of a husband here," Harriet said.

"A diamond," Marion agreed.

"Yes, the packaging is exceptional," Sandra said.

"What does that mean?" Harriet said, dragging her little boy out of the sandbox and preparing to leave the playground. Suddenly, they saw Roberta streak out of the Arms, yelling for the police.

Everyone jumped up and ran towards her. "Are you hurt, Bobbie? What happened?" Sandra asked, pulling her to a bench.

A haze of fear had wrapped around Roz, and she was incapable of talking.

"My mink stole, my diamond pin."

"Another one!" Marion gasped.

"Did they get that gold bracelet with the diamond clasp?"

"I don't know, Harriet." Bobbie waved her hands up and down frantically. "We need the police."

"You should have telephoned them from your apartment."

"What? Stay up there?"

"All right. We'll call from Mr. Fontanna's office," Sandra said and led Roberta away. The blonde, her long straight hair bobbing behind her, looked more than ever like a teenager to Roz who followed after them, wanting to help.

Harriet and Marion stopped at the elevator while the others went to the renting agent to report the burglary. "Her Jerome will have a fit," Roz heard Harriet say as she passed by. "I happen to know he bought everything on the installment plan."

In Mr. Fontanna's office, Roberta and Sandra waited while he called the precinct office. "And I want my lock changed right away," Roberta said. "I think the thief had a passkey."

"Is everyone who works in the building bonded?" Sandra asked.

"The doormen, the custodial staff, they've all been checked out."

"I don't care. Check them again. Someone has my mink stole and my diamond pin and I want them back."

Mr. Fontanna mopped his forehead with an initialed handkerchief. "Do me a favor, Mrs. Kramer and try to calm her. As it is, word will spread through the Arms like wildfire, but if she keeps screaming, the women will panic."

"Maybe they have reason to panic," Sandra said. "The burglaries continue, and it doesn't look like management is doing much to safeguard us."

"You should never know the aggravation I'm having with this mess. Everyone blames me, but I can't change all the locks three or four times a month."

"We've been robbed more often than that," Sandra said.

"It's the same in every luxury building. What can I do about it when you ladies like to keep your valuables at home?"

Thank goodness Marion had not come along, Roz thought. How would she stay alone in her apartment after this latest break-in? Perhaps I can offer to keep her company tonight or else Marty... No, Roz did not want Marty to see too much of her pretty cousin. Let Sandra or Neil do it.

Fotolia #57837082 - Subway Stop Downtown & Brooklyn New York City © anujakjaimook

The first time Neil held her was a bittersweet memory for Marion now.

Chapter 7

I t was nearly midnight when Marion woke from a nightmare. She'd dreamed that someone in a stocking mask sawed at the chain on the door to her apartment and after the first rush of relief on awakening, panicked at the idea of remaining alone. When it had happened before, she'd asked Sandra to stay with her. After a moment's hesitation, Marion called the Kramers.

Neil answered the telephone. "Sandra's dead to the world. I'd rather not get her out of bed."

His words reminded Marion how tired Sandra had been when they returned from the stores. She wanted to cry out to Neil that she couldn't bear to be alone but thanked him as calmly as possible and started to hang up.

"I'll be right down."

"You don't have to, Neil. Really."

"Just to check that everything's all right."

"Oh, Neil, would you?"

"Be there in a minute."

Marion scrambled out of bed and put on her turquoise robe. While in the bathroom combing her hair, she decided to brush her teeth. The doorbell rang as she finished and she looked through the peephole carefully, before letting Neil into the apartment.

"Old Neil will soon have the situation well in hand. Nothing to worry about."

"I hate living alone."

"Those clowns wouldn't try to break in while someone's home. They never do it that way."

Neil always cheered her, Marion thought, and wished Sandra would suddenly run off with the milkman and leave Neil free. But Sandra, who'd grabbed Neil only a few months after moving to Brooklyn, obviously knew a good thing when she saw it. And they seemed so happy. Marion had often noticed how tenderly he looked towards Sandra at unexpected moments.

"Would you like some coffee?" she asked to keep him there.

"Great."

He saw her hesitate at the doorway to the kitchen and seemed to understand immediately that Marion was still frightened. In a minute, he'd bounded to her side and had the kitchen flooded in fluorescent light. He made a pretense of checking the broom closet.

"I'm such a fool."

"It's good to see you laugh."

Marion knew her laughter was close to tears and turned away to fill the percolator. If Neil came nearer, she would cry and cling to him, unable to stop herself. When she plugged in the coffee pot, she noticed he leaned against the refrigerator, regarding her movements with interest.

"Do you still think about Alec?"

The question startled Marion, who had been wishing again that Neil were free. "All the time."

"I didn't mean that as stupidly as it sounded."

"It wasn't stupid."

"What I really meant was, do you think you'll ever fall in love again?"

"Do you want to throw your brother-in-law at me, too?"

"That's the last thing I want."

"Then why?"

Neil filled his pipe, giving it all of his attention. "It's not natural for you to be alone like this."

"Tell me something new."

Her sarcasm seemed to surprise Neil, and he was silent while she took two cups and saucers from her Rosenthal china and put them on the table.

"What lovely things you have," Neil said. "You've surrounded yourself with a perfect setting."

Marion remembered Mama's indignation at discovering Marion planned to keep only one set of dishes. "A trefe home. God forbid." But Marion had persisted, her stubbornness buoyed by the knowledge that two sets of Rosenthal, one for meat and one for dairy would be overwhelmingly expensive. She was glad now that she could use the best dishes for Neil rather than have them reserved for meat dinners the way it was at Mama's.

When Marion had placed sugar and cream on the table and had poured coffee for both of them, she invited Neil, who still lounged against the refrigerator, to sit down.

"How is your mother, Neil?" She'd heard from Sandra that morning about the old lady's bursitis.

"Not too bad. I hope she'll be well enough to take Toby when Sandra and I are ready to travel."

"Are you going to South America?" Marion could picture them arriving at Rio or Bahia, entertained in all the nightspots by the planters Neil bought coffee from, and dancing the tango or samba. Suddenly she saw herself in the scene instead of Sandra. What a fabulous life she'd have if Neil could take her to all those fascinating places.

"We'll see."

Three topics gone and the coffee hasn't even cooled enough to drink, Marion thought. He's so quiet tonight; maybe he's tired.

"Actually, Sandra wants to run up to the mountains."

"The Catskills?"

"Sure."

"But why go where everyone else does when you can really travel? Oh, Neil, you must put your foot down." He's a wonderful husband, Marion told herself again. He would do anything to please Sandra.

"Let's travel together. Imagine us in Bogotá or Rio," Neil said.

She upset her coffee and jumped up for a dishrag to clean the table but he took the cloth, put Marion in his own seat, and wiped the mess.

"You are jittery tonight; I'll stay awhile." After rinsing the cloth, Neil hung it neatly at the side of the kitchen sink. "My coffee's untouched. Drink it and I'll help myself to another cup."

He must think I'm a clumsy fool, Marion worried, but he's so tactful. When he left, she'd cherish his words in private even if they hadn't meant anything.

Neil now occupied her usual chair and she felt odd to face him from the opposite direction. From where she sat, Marion could see out into the dinette and living room, but Neil's view would be only of herself.

"I remember sitting here many evenings with Alec, solving all the world's problems while you and Sandra gabbed in the other room."

Marion ran out of the kitchen, pulling a tissue from her pocket as she went. In a moment, Neil was with her, stroking her back and soothing her.

"Hey, I didn't intend to make you cry."

He sat her down on the sofa, still holding her, and Marion who'd wanted to send him home, couldn't bear to do it.

"Feel better now?"

"Yes."

"Let me stay tonight."

Amid the dreamlike quality Neil's visit had taken on, Marion's senses whirled. She searched his face as if it held the answer for her. His blue-green eyes seemed to be staring at her with the same intensity.

"How about it, Marion? I've always wanted you." His caresses had changed from the comfort pats of a friend and neighbor, and he kissed her passionately.

Don't make me decide, she said to herself. Just act as though it were already settled.

"You need me."

Marion wanted to say yes, but the words stuck in her throat. He was marvelous. What was the point of circulating again and meeting anyone her friends pounced on for "poor Marion?" Sooner or later, she would find herself with a man she didn't even care for and sleep with him because of her unbearable loneliness. It would happen again and again until in desperation, she remarried. Some ordinary boor, she thought, and I'll be stuck for life.

"Marion."

Let it be Neil then. He, at least, meant something to her.

"Look at me, Marion."

Neil kissed her again and she clung to him. "Let me stay," he repeated.

Why not Neil! She was already half in love with him. She started to nod her head.

"Sandra will never know," he said.

"I tried to forget about Sandra. Now I can't do it," she cried.

"Sandra is sound asleep; I could be away for hours and not be discovered."

"Don't keep talking about her!"

"Whatever you want, Marion."

She disentangled herself and walked across the room. "It's time for you to go, Neil."

"You don't really want me to leave."

In reply, Marion removed the door chain and held open the door. She saw Neil lose his confidence for a moment, but when he left the apartment, he didn't seem disturbed.

"Goodnight." Neil blew her a kiss in his jaunty way and walked away.

Sandra doesn't need him the way 1 do, Marion thought. If only he had allowed it to seem unpremeditated, I could have quieted my conscience. These things happen all the time and no one is hurt.

Walking slowly into the kitchen, Marion busied herself clearing the cups and saucers from the table. A lot of good it did to wait until marriage last time, she reflected. I should have let him stay.

Towards morning, when Marion fell asleep, she dreamed Neil had returned but instead of making love to her, he ransacked the apartment.

How much she'd wanted Neil then; how little she really knew him.

Chapter 8

All morning, Marion kept to her apartment, drinking stale coffee left in the percolator from the night before, hoping Sandra wouldn't come down to visit her. Insisting to herself she hadn't harmed Sandra did no good. In high school and college merely dating someone else's "steady" was a serious crime. If only Neil were Harriet's husband or Roberta's, she could stifle her conscience more easily.

Marion wondered what the neighbors would have thought had they seen Neil leaving her apartment well after midnight. For that matter, she told herself, we could be together during the day, less innocently, and no one would ever know. The memory of Neil begging to spend the night with her sent a rush of excitement through Marion. When she finally began to dress, the mirror reflected sparkling gray eyes instead of the listless ones that had stared back at her for months. But she must forget last night and get back to the old relationship of neighbors and friends with Neil and Sandra.

By noon, Marion could stand her reflections no longer and caught the bus to Mama and Aunt Lena's.

"So she comes to see her Mama, finally."

"I was here Saturday."

"In and out like plucking a chicken."

"Mama, please."

"You are not fooling me." Her mother wore one of many flowered housedresses; this one, in shades of brown and tan, blended her into the beige walls of the apartment. Hair that had been dark brown, almost black, now showed mostly gray. For one guilt-filled moment, Marion wondered how much of that gray she'd caused.

"I'm not trying to fool you, Mama." Marion walked aimlessly around her mother's living room, peering at herself in the huge mirror over the brown tweed sofa. "Did you get the television fixed?"

"Don't change by me the subject. I know what you and your shiksa friend are up to."

From previous discussions, Marion knew that her "shiksa friend" was Sandra, another of Mama's unreasonable ideas. It was useless to repeat the information that Sandra was Jewish because her mother insisted that a girl from upstate who didn't keep kosher and who had named her son Toby was a "shiksa."

"Is Aunt Lena home?"

"Your aunt is in the grocery, getting for me some sugar." Marion's mother started for the kitchen at the first whistle of the tea kettle and Marion followed her. The big kitchen was overpoweringly hot in contrast to Marion's own air-conditioned apartment, but her mother sat down at the table, surrounded by clutter. What appeared to be old envelopes used for shopping lists and memos, and a collection of paper bags overspread a good part of the table.

"It's too hot for tea, Mama."

"What do you think? Am I Tante Sarah? Eleven years ago, your father and I visited one afternoon and she did not even offer us anything to eat. Not so much as a glass of tea, if you can imagine it."

Marion had heard the story of this offense committed by some distant relation of her father many times before and knew she couldn't escape the tea. She puffed a long breath of air through her magenta lips and tried to seem as if she listened.

"Take out the cups, Marion, but don't mix up."

"After all these years, I know which ones are the dairy dishes." Actually, it wasn't easy as nothing matched and Marion sometimes wanted to smash every dish in the place so that her mother would have to use the untouched sets she kept packed away, the ones saved because they were too good to use.

"Oh, my daughter's so smart, but does she know to stay away from the shiksa's brother?"

Here we go, Marion thought.

"A shame, it is."

"Don't get steamed up, Mama. I'm not interested in Sandra's brother."

"My daughter comes to see me last Saturday and not a word about the big appointment."

"Then how did you know?"

"Sooner or later all the dirt comes out in the wash."

"Come on, Mama. Who told you about my date?"

"Your cousin just happened to mention it."

"If there's anything I don't need, it's a spy in my building." Marion ignored the steaming cup of tea, wondering if she dared to go to the refrigerator and use ice cubes to transform it into iced tea.

"Do you have something to hide?"

You'd really get upset if you knew, Marion said to herself and remembered to cover her smile in time.

"Marion, you look wonderful." Aunt Lena let herself into the apartment and brought her packages to the kitchen. Unlike Mama with her closet of housedresses, Aunt Lena wore navy slacks with a paisley blouse. She kissed Marion's cheek and Marion impulsively hugged her until she felt her mother's sadness that the aunt should be greeted with joy but the mother visited as a duty.

"Your face is alive," Aunt Lena said. "So, you must have met a young man."

"Not really."

Aunt Lena sat down and poured herself a cup of tea. "I can tell."

"Looking at me you know there's a new man on the scene?" Marion tried to make it sound like commentary on Aunt Lena's words rather than the delightful knowledge that Neil wanted her.

"Who is it?"

"Lena, you say that I am the one with imagination. My daughter looks the same to me as always."

"Who is he?" Aunt Lena repeated.

"If only he weren't married to Sandra," Marion blurted.

"A married man!" Mama screamed.

"He could get a divorce."

"I brought her up in a good Jewish home," Mama moaned.

"Calm down, Bertha," Aunt Lena said. "You're shrieking loud enough to bring the neighbors."

"A divorce would mean we could marry."

"No divorces in this family," Mama shouted. "Not even a Get, a Jewish divorce."

"Would you rather we had an affair?" She was furious at her mother's opposition to an idea still far from reality and yet, Marion realized, she had come here today to sound out Mama and Aunt Lena.

"I never heard such talk. Are you trying to kill me?"

Mama sat down again clutching her chest with both hands.

"Your heart's as good as mine," Aunt Lena said. "Why don't you keep quiet and let Marion live her own life?"

"No wonder the girl is wild."

"Does he care for you, too?"

Marion took her time, wondering what to answer Aunt Lena. If she said Neil felt the same way, either Mama or her aunt would ask how she knew and the story of last night would be out, despite any attempt to withhold it. It's none of their business, she thought. Sharing Neil's kisses could make them seem less important. What did it really mean, anyhow?

Perhaps he only wanted to seize the opportunity, believing the old tale that divorcées and widows were especially vulnerable. As she was.

"Some mothers can trust their daughters."

"And some daughters..."

"All right. You're both too old for these arguments."

If Aunt Lena didn't stop them, Marion feared the long silent subject would emerge. She'd been ready to yell that Mama had lost her right to be heard.

Aunt Lena glanced at Marion. "Does your friend know?"

"I don't think so."

"Don't let her stand in your way. You have suffered enough."

"I'm so mixed up." Not for the first time, Marion wondered whether the modern outlook of her widowed aunt had included lovers of her own.

"If you want him, get him while you can."

"My own sister talks like this? I could die to hear it."

"Bertha, the girl deserves her chance for happiness."

"Happiness! Today everyone wants instant happiness without responsibility."

The doorbell rang before Bertha Benjamin could continue the argument and she went to answer it. While she was out of the room, Marion turned to her aunt.

"Please help me." Now that her emotions had been voiced, they were no longer fantasies but more like future plans.

"You know that I am on your side, always."

"But what shall I do?"

"Forget about friendship and act as if he were any young man you wanted to marry."

"I don't want a complete break with Mama."

"Don't worry. I'll handle your mother."

"Maybe I should have made the break right after the accident," Marion told Aunt Lena, knowing as she spoke that it could be much easier now but would have been impossible then. Mama had been lying in the hospital, recovering from her stroke and Marion had to conquer her own grief and visit the hospital every day.

"Look who is here," Mama said, leading Roz Geller into the kitchen.

"Oh, Marion. I wish I knew you were coming here. We could have traveled together on the bus."

"I didn't decide until the last minute. I just had to get out."

"Staying home alone is not pleasant."

"You have Marty," Marion said, immediately sorry. She didn't want pity from Roz, especially in front of Mama and Aunt Lena. "How are you getting along? All settled?"

"We do not have much furniture, but we manage."

"Today the children want to start with all it took the parents a lifetime to get," Mama commented. "First the television and the bed, then they buy everything else."

"Our apartment is very expensive. We must wait."

"And how are your neighbors, Roslyn?"

"Mama, you've lived here long enough to know that the neighbors don't give a damn."

"Such talk. Roslyn, do you speak like that to your mother?"

"You'd think I was ten years old," Marion said and wondered how long before she could make her escape.

"I have been a refugee twice, Cousin Bertha. It is not easy to make friends."

"You've met a few of the girls from our building," Marion said, annoyed at Roz for making her feel guilty. She had too many problems of her own to take any trouble for her cousin.

"Plenty of rich ones in that place," Aunt Lena said.

"I think that some only pretend."

"How can you say that? We have dress manufacturers, importers, lawyers, accountants, jewelers. Lots of people with money at the Arms. Why in apartment 4A, they put down a seven hundred dollar marble floor in the foyer. And the couple in 2L paid thousands for their carpeting."

"What a waste of money just to step in comfort."

"If they didn't have it, Mama, they wouldn't be able to spend it."

"Roslyn, sit over here and I will get you some tea."

"I'll take care of it, Mama." Marion felt a twinge of envy to see Mama willing to wait on her cousin.

"Is he handsome?" Aunt Lena suddenly asked.

Marion glanced at Roz out of the corner of her eye and blushed, glad the girl had missed the first part of the conversation and the scene that had followed. With luck, she could answer Aunt Lena without giving herself away.

"Wonderful."

"Does he make a good living?"

"Sure."

"Anyhow, you have the insurance money from Alec."

"Aunt Lena, please."

"You may not like to think about the money, but it was a blessing he left you without financial worries." Aunt Lena took off one of the tiny diamond earrings she always wore. "This is all your uncle left me."

Were there memories as well, Marion wondered, or was her aunt too old to remember? Perhaps it was true that all memories faded with time, but older people said much she'd found wasn't so.

"Don't let your Mama keep you from marrying again. She will get used to the idea."

"I knew he was the right one," Roz said. "I am so happy for you."

How did she find out? Did everyone know? Marion was frightened, knowing if gossip reached Sandra, she would soon find herself committed irrevocably before making up her mind.

"And he is a teacher. It is so wonderful."

"You mean Eddie Berg." Marion stood up in disgust.

"Don't go. Have more tea," Bertha Benjamin said to her daughter.

"I have to get back, Mama."

"So the husbands will wait another hour for you to snatch them."

"Leave the girl alone."

"That is the trouble. We have left her alone to do as she pleases for too long now."

Marion remained standing, staring down at her mother without knowing what to say to make her understand. "Life is too short for me to waste time."

"But why this?"

"I want something different, Mama. Surely, life must offer more than sitting in the playground and discussing which babies are teething."

"For the other women, it is good enough?"

"You'll never understand. If the marriage were happy, would there be any chance for me? And if it's not happy, then why should three of us waste our lives?" It was one of the arguments Marion had used on herself that morning.

Roz looked from one to the other as she slowly sipped her tea. "Eddie is married?"

All right, you asked for it, Marion thought. If she wanted her second chance, she must toughen up and this was a good time to start. "We were talking about Neil Kramer."

For an instant, when she saw the color leave Roz' face, Marion felt sorry. But it was too early to quit; she'd been through worse than this without giving up. Nothing might come of her interest in Neil, but she would establish the right to live without her family's interference. Luckily, Alec's parents now lived in California, and her relationship with them consisted only of a yearly exchange of Hebrew New Year cards. If she were to remarry, perhaps the cards would stop, but there'd be no other indication of disapproval from that direction.

"Is what the women say true, then?" Roz asked. "About you and Neil."

"It's not possible for you to have heard about us, because nothing happened."

"Eddie is much finer than Neil."

"You must have noticed at the dinner party how dazzling Neil is. I'll never meet anyone else like him."

Marion saw that Roz wanted to dispute this but she couldn't allow her cousin any further chance to discuss Neil in front of Mama and Aunt Lena. She started out of the kitchen, planning to throw quick goodbyes to everyone from the hallway, but Roz's hurt expression stopped her momentarily.

"I really did mean to look after you. I'll introduce you to more people in the building."

"Better it should be the other way around," Mama said.

"Please do not worry, Cousin Bertha."

"You keep an eye on my daughter, she should not do foolish things," Mama said loudly as Marion started for the front door.

Fotolia #62414503 - Brooklyn Bridge @ Brooklyn; Manhattan Br in background © vivalapenler

Roz apologized to her repeatedly, but it was a long time before Marion forgave her cousin and even longer before she wished she'd listened to her.

Chapter 9

In the end, Roz made hurried excuses to Cousin Bertha and Cousin Lena and ran after Marion. The street was hot and noisy. Children on skateboards careened past Roz, the din adding to her confusion. The neighborhood, an old one with trees along both sides of the street and stately apartment houses, had boasted the luxury buildings of their day. Although the building façades were now dingy, it remained a pleasant-looking neighborhood, and Roz thought how good it would be to live here and not worry about the expense of the Mediterranean Arms.

As she rushed through the streets to the bus stop, Roz realized the neighbors were right, and her stomach tightened. She understood now that Marion was interested in Sandra's husband, and her own insecure fears about Marty were groundless. But for Cousin Bertha's sake, she determined to dissuade Marion.

"I've had it today. Leave me alone." Marion said before Roz uttered a word. "And don't tell anyone in our building that my aunt and my mother live in such a rundown placc, either."

For a moment, Roz wanted to avoid the subject but Marion was family. "You do not want my opinion, but ..."

"You're right. It's nobody's business but my own."

"And that of all the women in our building."

"What do you mean?"

"You are serious about Neil Kramer?"

After digging into her handbag for fare, Marion stepped off the curb to look past the row of parked cars. "This is the slowest bus line in the city."

Patiently, Roz waited until it became obvious Marion had no intention of returning to the subject. She must plunge forward again. "What is wrong with the brother?"

"Nothing. I'm going out with him again this weekend."

"You will know him better and find that he is a better man than Neil Kramer."

"Except that he has no sex appeal."

The other girl's words, so blunt, jolted Roz. When she'd lived in Florida, a classmate named Sue Ellen had sometimes tried to shock her, but Roz learned not to react.

"Neil Kramer has only sex appeal. There is nothing more to him."

The bus arrived. They pushed past people who exited inconsiderately from the front door and held onto the backs of two adjacent seats, ready to grab them when their occupants left the bus. Private conversation was impossible now but Roz mulled over what she would say later.

When they left the bus, her chance came as they stood on the corner waiting for the traffic light to change. "In our building, the women are betting how long it will take you to get Neil."

"I don't believe you."

"They told this to me the very first day."

Marion put her hands up as if to shield her face, but immediately recovered herself. One pair of gray eyes pierced the other's dark ones. "You're crazy."

"I am telling the truth."

"Mama wanted you to talk to me."

"It is my own idea."

"What does a newlywed know about my problems? I can't go on this way. Every day is the same since Alec died— nothing to look forward to but getting through the hours until it's time to fall asleep again. Why can't people mind their own business?"

"We are worried about you, Marion."

"I want excitement and glamour again and Neil is the only one who can make it happen."

"There will be excitement in getting him but after that is over—nothing."

"I played it straight the first time, with Alec, and it only led to misery. You don't know anything about it, Roz. Don't judge me."

"Finish. Say that I am only a displaced person. That is a good expression. It is like calling the poor 'disadvantaged,' which does not make them any richer."

"I'm sorry. I didn't intend to hurt you."

"You Americans are always so polite. True friends do not smile at each other all the time; they are frank. They say what they mean. You are not sorry."

Marion, silent, stared at her cousin and realized for the first time how pretty the younger girl was despite her old-fashioned hairdo. Her eyes, a dark shade of brown that seemed almost black, were part of her attractiveness—but Roz's caring, kindhearted expression did even more for her looks. Right now, though, the latter was annoying to Marion.

"You're married to an American now," Marion said finally, feeling sympathy for her cousin's insecurity. "The past is over."

"It will never be behind me," Roz said, "all my life, I will feel lesser, apart from the accepted ones."

They stood in front of the Mediterranean Arms now, but no one passed by and they remained out of earshot of the doorman, who had opened the door wide at sighting them but let it close again when they made no move to approach.

"Your past has nothing to do with my personal life. Surely you realize that, Roz."

"Your mother helped us then; I want to help her now. I know little about furniture and clothes, as you have observed, but I do know people. I have had to understand people in order to exist."

"Please drop it, Roz."

"At first Neil impressed me, too. When I realized his charm is only superficial, I thought the mistake was mine." Her own husband had once seemed to Roz like all the other brash New York know-it-alls who flew down to Miami Beach on two-week vacations, and on the surface he was. In Neil Kramer, however, the bravado wasn't confined to the surface, to his speech and mannerisms; there was nothing else.

"Every woman in our building is crazy about Neil. You're just jealous," Marion said and turned away.

"No."

"I notice the way you look at my furniture and dresses and the way you couldn't help mentioning them just now."

"Come upstairs where we can speak more. I must make you understand."

"Leave me alone."

"Marty will tell you the same. He sees it, too."

"He wishes that he had an exciting career like Neil instead of being a clerk in some little office. You make me sick." Marion started toward the front door, past the white marble sculptures.

"Wait!"

"I won't sacrifice my life to please you."

"And you do not care what the women will say about you?"

"If Neil were single, no one would say a word." Marion took a few more steps and turned around again. "And you can report whatever you like to Mama."

Roz walked past the front of the building and on to the park, feeling very ineffectual. She had never been able to stand up to anyone. When she guessed that her cousin had enough time to reach the elevator and go to her own apartment, she returned to the lobby. She had no time to waste if she wanted to have dinner ready when Marty arrived from work.

As Roz started the hamburgers broiling, she heard Marty's key in the lock and ran to the door. "You look so uncomfortable."

"You try riding the subway in the rush hour on a day like today."

"I went only on the bus to Cousin Bertha."

Marty sat down directly in front of the air conditioning unit. "This is worth all the money we pay for the apartment." He stretched out his arms for her and she sat on his lap. "Wouldn't feel like this without the air conditioner. What did the old lady have to say?"

"She is upset because of Marion."

"That girl could agitate anyone; she has too much animal magnetism."

"You like Marion?"

"Don't worry. I'm not looking for trouble." Marty walked over to the table at Roz's insistence that dinner was ready, although he said he would prefer sitting in front of the air conditioner until thoroughly chilled. She told him about her quarrel with Marion.

"Why the hell are you butting in?"

"She is my cousin."

"So?"

"She will ruin her life."

"That's her hard luck. You stay out of it."

Roz added ketchup to her hamburger and chewed it carefully while she tried out words to make Marty understand. Although he insisted that she spoke English well, Roz sometimes felt that he did not really hear her.

"How are the two old ladies? You enjoy going over there?" Marty asked.

"Cousin Bertha likes to see me, but today it was not very pleasant. She asked me to keep an eye on Marion."

"Don't you get mixed up in it."

"I do not know what to do. I owe much to Cousin Bertha, but I cannot spy on Marion."

"Forget it, Roz."

"Cousin Bertha helped my family when we needed her."

"I know all about that, but what I said goes double. Stay out of it."

When Marty became gruff, Roz knew it was time to change the subject but couldn't drop this one. She stood and walked over to his side of the table. "If only I could make Marion understand what I see."

"Keep away from her. Your cousin is like a time bomb waiting to go off, and I don't want you caught in the blast." He pounded on the table overturning a bottle of Pepsi Cola. Roz quickly wiped up the mess. The dinette area of their apartment was a corner of the living room; a spill on the parquet floor was more damaging than one on vinyl tile.

"It is good that we have no carpet."

"We'll get the damn carpeting. We'll get everything the others have."

"I did not mean it that way. Please Marty, we must not quarrel."

"I'm not arguing. I told you not to do something and I mean it. All of a sudden, I don't count. Everything is Cousin Bertha this and Marion that."

"I thought that you liked Marion."

"Look, Roz," Marty said in a calmer tone; "I'm sorry, but she's not your sister, you know. She's only a distant cousin. Living in the same building doesn't mean we have to be involved with her affairs. I moved here to come up in the world."

"I do not understand you."

"There's going to be trouble and we're not taking sides. Now do you get it?"

Roz, who should have been relieved to realize Marty had no interest in her lovely cousin, found herself filled with worry because they'd quarreled. She wondered whether other couples in the building argued or if the women had only to stretch out slim, manicured hands to end any dissension. Once she'd dreamed that she could be like the wealthy visitors to

Miami Beach if she married an American but now Roz knew she could never compete with them.

"Don't look so sad; you make me feel like a heel."

"I am not sad."

"You're sure not the picture of sunshine."

"It is only that I expected life to become easier."

Marty walked around to Roz' side of the table and took up a stance behind her chair, putting his arms around both chair and Roz's waist. "If you expect nothing but good days, you'll soon be like all the spoiled women here."

"All my life has been hard."

"Don't compare today with yesterday, Roz, but with five years ago and ten years ago. You're happier now."

Roz brightened with pleasure knowing she hadn't been wrong about Marty. The habit of doing everything for show, for the impression it would make on neighbors or the people he worked with, all of this was the superficial Marty. She alone knew him as a perceptive, tender husband. This was what she'd meant to explain to Marion when she tried to point out the difference between Neil Kramer and his brother-in-law. What insight would Neil have into Marion's problems if she were ever unhappy? Roz suddenly wanted to rush downstairs to her cousin's apartment and try to convince her before it was too late, but she couldn't do it in the face of Marty's opposition. She was not yet that Americanized.

"Feel better?" Marty asked.

Roz tilted her head so she could look up at her husband. "We should never have moved into this building. It will be bad for us. I feel it."

"I like it here," he said and lifted her into his arms.

Fotolia #69030946 - Brooklyn old buildings and Manhattan Bridge in Dumbo © blvdone

That long-ago outing with Eddie had alleviated her loneliness for a little while and Marion had hated to see the day end, but she was determined not to be attracted to him.

Chapter 10

As it was Memorial Day weekend, Eddie decided on an early start for Connecticut. Marion was ready when he arrived for their date. For warm weather comfort, she wore a simple sage-green linen dress but carried a lightweight wrap in case the weather changed as it often did in late spring.

The rush of air through the car windows made Marion feel alive and she thought how pleasant it was to leave the city for the day, even with Eddie. Neither one had much to say as they rode along the Belt Parkway to the Van Wyck Expressway.

"I haven't been in the Bronx for years," Marion said when they crossed the Whitestone Bridge.

"It looks just like Brooklyn to me."

"You must be joking. I wouldn't live up here for anything."

"You Brooklynites are like Texans. You'd be happy nowhere else in the world. Paris, Rome, Madrid, all interludes until you could get back to Brooklyn."

Marion was furious. "You're wrong," she said. "If I could travel, I'd be tremendously happy."

"No one's stopping you. For the money you women spend on clothes, you could easily fly to Europe."

"Alone, that's the catch."

"Well, lamb, when my trip to Spain becomes a reality, I'll take you along."

Marion didn't answer him. She was daydreaming about going to South America with Neil; it could be their honeymoon. You little fool, she told herself, that may be furthest from Neil's mind.

"There's the Connecticut Turnpike," Eddie said. "I guess we'd save time on it, but I like the Merritt Parkway better. More scenic, less rush. It's just an old-fashioned rolling highway."

How romantic to ramble on about roads, Marion thought. No wonder I can't get excited about him. And when did he get a chance to travel this way before. He must have been down from Syracuse many times, but Sandra never bothered to have us meet while I was married.

"When we get off the Parkway, keep your eyes open for signs advertising antiques," Eddie reminded Marion. But he spotted an antique shop first.

They wandered around, lifting pieces to see the markings, asking questions and browsing. Eddie didn't appear enthusiastic about anything, and Marion tried not to seem unsophisticated by showing too much interest until she came across a painting of a man and woman sitting at the water's edge, feeding swans.

"Look at that, Eddie. It matches my drapes."

Eddie just gazed at her with his intent stare until she flushed and turned away. "Let's have lunch now," he said.

"That sounds good." Marion hoped he would take her to a nice place this time, not because she wanted to spend his money but for the pleasure of dining there with a man. She was beginning to understand why rich, old ladies paid for escorts.

"Ah, this looks good." It was a small, bright restaurant with a "Pizza" sign over the doorway. Marion knew they would find red-and-white checked tablecloths, probably oilcloth. It was that kind of place. She let Eddie order a huge pizza with cheese, mushrooms, onions, and green pepper and had two slices herself. He kept urging her to eat more.

"You sound like Mama. 'Eat, Marion.'"

"All right. I've been told off."

"I didn't mean to hurt your feelings."

"Don't worry, I save hurt feelings for more important issues, like when I ask a girl to sleep with me."

"Everybody thinks a widow is fair game."

"Hold it down to a shout, will you?"

"Look, Eddie." But she stopped, because she saw that he was laughing at her again.

"I figured that would get a rise out of you," he said. "You look very prim today."

"You're having plenty of fun at my expense."

"Not really. I enjoy being with you, Marion."

She knew that Eddie waited to hear a similar declaration from her but she couldn't do it; the words would stick in her throat. Why did I come here with him, she asked herself. He only complicates my life.

"People fall into little ruts," Eddie was saying. "Before you know it, your vocabulary decreases, your outlook narrows and what remains? When the mah jong, bridge parties, and organization meetings are done, you glance back at your life and wonder what it was all about."

"Are you trying to say that I'm wasting my life?"

"I'm saying that many women do. But you can answer the question better than I can. Aren't you?"

"And if I go home with you, it won't be wasted?" Marion asked as sarcastically as she could.

"Depends how you define 'it'," Eddie said.

"Go ahead, laugh at me." But even as she spoke, Marion knew he used humor to soften her refusal.

"We could head right back to Brooklyn."

"You've got a nerve. Two slices of pizza and a drive in a borrowed car and you expect me to fall into bed with you," she said despite her resolve to let him down easy.

"No lamb, I thought you might be lonely, too."

"I am, but not that lonely."

"Good."

"You're a strange person."

"As I told you before, I'm old-fashioned. I wanted you to refuse."

"If that's a line," Marion said, "it's the best I've heard."

"How cynical you are."

They'd finished the pizza and Eddie surprised her by ordering cheese cake and coffee for both of them, again without consulting her. He bewildered her with a swift change from teasing to a lecture. "Take note, when man is concerned with woman's virtue, man is interested in that woman."

Marion refrained from the trite, "I barely know you," and smiled at him instead, walking the tightrope between kindness and encouragement. While it was flattering to hear that he cared for her, she was in no mood for further turbulence. Eddie was someone to talk to, someone who helped a day pass more quickly, but you couldn't explain that to a man without making him feel like a pet Pekingese. The picture of a Pekingese with Eddie's face flashed into Marion's mind and she giggled.

"I don't know what that's all about, but you have a delightful smile. Did you know your nose wrinkles?"

Eddie paid the check, leaving a twenty-five cent tip and took Marion's hand as they walked back to the car. She hated his cheapness and tried to ignore it.

Their next stop was an antique store with a painted sign on the window guaranteeing that nothing less than fifty years old was sold there.

"I'll bet we can pick up a real bargain in this place. And all the stuff is guaranteed."

"How can you fall for that?"

Without understanding his tone, Marion was reminded of his sister. "Can't we go in?"

"We'll do whatever you like, but I want you to realize that fifty years doesn't make an antique. When I'm teaching, it always surprises me to remember that World War II,

Hiroshima, the Berlin Blockade all happened before the time of my students. And I'm not that much older than they are."

Another lecture. What was the matter with him? And Sandra was exactly the same. She should have become a teacher, too.

"Don't let advertising confuse you, Marion. Use your brains instead of allowing them to atrophy. No woman who did well enough on the entrance exam to Hunter College and got her degree there can be as shallow as you pretend to be."

Marion swallowed her anger. What was the point of ruining their day?

In the end, they walked into the shop, and she glanced quickly at Eddie to see whether he was impressed with the style of the displays. Showcases were lined with red velvet and the bigger pieces were on raised stands making very attractive settings. She showed Eddie a figurine that interested her, a boy and girl in Bavarian dress.

"You can buy that in the five and ten."

"Shhh. He'll hear you." Marion nodded toward the proprietor.

"Now here's something worthwhile."

She opened her hand to accept what he held out, a gold and cloisonné box. Lovely workmanship, but after the first moment when she assumed it was a cigarette case, Marion couldn't figure out what it was for.

"Recognize this? A Havdalah spicebox. There's the little drawer for the spices and some Hebrew letters." He must have noticed the blank look on Marion's face. "Sandra told me that you come from a religious home."

"I never knew that you did."

"Orthodox Jews from New York City think there's none elsewhere." Eddie reached for the Havdalah box again. "You'll remember the Havdalah ceremony in a minute. Think of Saturday night when Shabbos is over and three stars are seen in the sky. There's the wine cup filled until it overflows to symbolize the fullness of blessings, the braided candle

because the world began with light, and the spices to promise
the start of a fragrant week."

Well, Mama would certainly approve of him, Marion
thought. Strange that Sandra was an unobservant Jew while
you could hear the emotional pull of the religion in her
brother's voice, even though he obviously was no longer a
Sabbath observer or they wouldn't be riding around
Connecticut today.

"I vaguely remember when my father was alive, going
with him to synagogue on Friday night or Saturday morning.
My father loved the services." Marion turned the spice box
over in her hand, fingering the intricate design. "I think I'd
like to have this."

"Let me buy it for you."

She started to refuse, but Eddie had taken it to the
proprietor for wrapping and a few moments later, handed it to
Marion, silver-papered and bowed; all she could do was
accept the gift graciously.

"We should start back; traffic will be tight."

When they were on the Merritt Parkway again heading
south to New York, Marion felt grateful she'd enjoyed a day
different from all the others since Alec's death. It wasn't
Eddie's fault that she would've preferred being with his
brother-in-law.

"You're quiet today. What are you thinking about?"

"Nothing."

"With that sensuous look?"

Marion covered her cheeks with both hands. How did he
know? Don't be silly, she told herself. He has no idea which
end is up. Now that was a picturesque expression. One Neil
liked to use, she remembered.

"You wouldn't have much trouble getting him, but he
isn't worth it."

She was honest enough not to ask Eddie what he was
talking about though it took tremendous effort.

"I like to study people. When I saw the way you looked at Neil the first time we met—at dinner in their apartment—I could see you were infatuated."

"That's why you started dating me?"

"Yes, lamb. In the beginning, I had some gallant idea of helping my sister."

"It's been nice but let's forget the whole thing now." They had entered heavy traffic, not gaining much mileage, and she could see that the trip, which had taken about two-and-a-half hours to Connecticut, would be much longer on the return leg.

"I'd like to see you again next weekend."

"But you just admitted the reason you've been dating me."

"That was how it began."

"And this is how it ends."

"Don't be flip. You're really not like that."

"Must you delude yourself?"

Eddie sighed audibly. The cars were bumper-to-bumper at the approach to the Bronx-Whitestone Bridge, and he could turn to look at her. "That's a good word, but it applies to you, not me. Do you know the story about the Emperor and his nightingale?"

"I think I lost you someplace."

"The fairy tale. Where the real nightingale is banished in favor of a handsome jewelled imitation."

"And you're the genuine article."

"I've never been compared to a nightingale before but in this context, yes. And Neil, to put it in terms that will be unmistakable to you, is the phony."

"You're very sure of yourself."

"On the contrary."

"You surely give an impression of self-confidence."

"It's a long time since I've met someone I wanted to see again and again. I'm not giving up easily."

Marion had no reply and Eddie remained quiet, also. Instead of the dismay Marion knew she should feel, she was conscious of pride in creating a potential storm center. She wondered whether Sandra considered the poor little widow a threat, that what Sandra had was not necessarily permanent, either. Even if Marion made no move to get Neil, she would know she could have done it. Eddie certainly considered it possible.

"This traffic is awful. Are you all right?"

"Just a little thirsty."

"I wanted to take you to a Havdalah service tonight but we'll never make it."

"Don't you think it would be better not to see each other again?"

Eddie took her hand and held it while he kept the other one on the wheel and his eyes carefully on the road. "We don't always do what's sensible. You should know that. Next Saturday, I have a business appointment, but I'll pick you up Sunday night at eight thirty. We can have dinner and dance at one of the little places on the Island."

"No, there's no point to that."

"You're going to stay out of trouble, Marion, if I have to make a scene in the lobby of your fancy building next Sunday."

Marion noticed two little boys on the playground swings, and her mind suddenly flashed on Sandra and Neil's sweet little Toby. She had grown to love him but always felt Toby deserved better than she could give him.

Chapter 11

They all have advice to offer me, Marion thought bitterly, but she wanted more from life than the ordinary existence that satisfied her neighbors. She had begun to believe again that something special was in the offing. The problem was whether to try actively for Neil, as everyone expected, or continue to drift. When Sandra invited her to the beach the Monday of Memorial Day, Marion had not yet made up her mind.

"Neil went into the office to clear up some unfinished work."

"You're going alone?"

"I have to take Toby along. I promised him."

Marion, who didn't relish spending the day with a four-year-old, wanted to decline. Unfortunately, all of her friends with the exception of former classmates scattered throughout the city and the Island whom she saw a couple of times a year, lived in the Arms. If she didn't go with Sandra, she would have to spend the day alone.

Her fantasies about Neil made it difficult to be comfortable with his wife but Sandra's manner was so relaxed, Marion decided she suspected nothing.

They chose Manhattan Beach and walked along the streets in bathing suits and beach robes, floppy sun hats and sunglasses, carrying aluminum folding chairs and straw baskets to hold all the odds and ends needed for a day in the sun. Although the beach was a short walk from the Mediterranean Arms, once they staked out a spot near the ocean, they would remain for hours and not bother returning either for lunch or forgotten items.

"I love these homes," Sandra said. The streets fronting Manhattan Beach had some of the finest custom-built homes in Brooklyn. Duplication was rare here unlike the rest of the borough where row homes were commonplace.

"I wouldn't give up my apartment for any one of them."

"Where I come from, we all had houses. It just tickles me the way people here call them 'private homes.' We didn't have to say that; every house was a 'private home.'"

"But look what we have—a doorman, a beautiful lobby, the playground, air conditioning."

"I'd change them for a house in a minute," Sandra said. "Even an attached house."

"Are you really that homesick?" Some people never know when they're well off, Marion thought.

They had arrived at the beach and started towards the ocean. "God, it's crowded today!"

"Good thing we didn't go to Brighton," Sandra said. "I was thinking Bay Two might be nice."

"All you need is to pick up fellows at Bay Two."

"Since when are you so prudish, Sandra?"

"And since when are you so silly."

"Mommy, mommy. I left my biggest, bestest shovel home." Toby kicked up sand as he ran along; his bright red bathing shorts were already covered in sand and within minutes, he'd rubbed sandy fingers into his curly blond hair.

What a day we're going to have, Marion thought, but Sandra turned to the boy and calmly told him that after lunch he could have the top of a plastic container to use as a scoop.

"But I need it now."

"Now it's covering the potato salad, but as soon as we finish eating, Mommy will give it to you."

"You have tremendous patience," Marion said.

"Either I talk this way to Toby or I'll end up screaming like most of the gals in our building. Did you ever notice they yell at their kids constantly? I just don't care to bring him up that way."

"Yet you leave him with sitters all the time."

"I'm not a possessive parent; I don't have to be with my son twenty-four hours a day to be a good mother. I could leave Toby tomorrow and take a trip to South America without worrying what it would do to his little psyche."

"I don't know much about kids."

"If you and Alec had had children, you'd be better off now."

"I wouldn't know what to do with a child."

"You'd learn."

"And make a mess of the job like Mama did."

"Are you looking for compliments, Marion? Your mother didn't do as badly as you believe."

They walked as close to the ocean as they could get, stepping over other people's blankets, toys and feet, following a barely discernible trail of empty space. When they found a spot large enough to spread a blanket for Toby and set up the webbed chairs, there were still people in front of them, but they couldn't get much closer to the ocean. Toby ran to the edge of the water and started building mud castles while his mother went in for a swim. A few minutes after she followed Sandra in, Marion decided the water was too cold and started back to her chair.

"Come on, it's delightful."

"Not for me."

"You won't melt. Come on."

"Don't be playful, Sandra. I'm old enough to know whether I want to swim."

"So touchy," Sandra said before she turned away and took her son into the ocean. From her chair, Marion could see them splashing around. The ice cream man came by and after a while another boy selling pretzels, but Marion had become absorbed in a crossword puzzle and didn't notice when her friend returned. The noises of the beach formed a background buzz in her head and she became aware of it only when a teenager with transistorized rock and roll passed by or when some mother dragged a howling child past her chair.

"I've worked up an appetite." Sandra fished around in her straw bag. "Want some salami?"

"No thanks; I've got corned beef." Absentmindedly, Marion chewed her own sandwich and topped it off with a peach. Toby gulped his salami and a soft drink before he ran back to play in the mud. Once he was gone, Marion knew her friend would question her about the two dates with Eddie.

"My brother says he can really talk to you."

"I used to freeze on dates but now I'm not worried about impressing anyone, so I can relax and be myself."

"It seems to work with Eddie."

"That's the strange part. The effect is to attract men."

"Don't I know it."

Marion glanced up quickly but the remark seemed without malice. If she guessed Neil is interested, Marion told herself, she wouldn't hesitate to tell me off. No girl is less devious than Sandra.

"Mommy."

"Just a minute, Toby."

"But mommy."

"I'm still talking to Mrs. Davis."

"But I threw up."

As Sandra hurried over to the place where Toby had been playing, Marion restrained herself from running home. How could Sandra, the daintiest of all her neighbors, stand it?

"Not too bad. It must have been all that soda on top of the salami."

"Shall we go home?"

"Don't look so upset or the same thing will happen to you. Everything's under control."

"Maybe he's coming down with something," Marion suggested.

"Could be. I'll let his daddy worry about that this evening."

Marion concluded her friend was relaxed to the point of callousness. After her own apron-stringed childhood, she never could've been a calm mother. No wonder little children frightened her.

"We were talking about Eddie," Sandra said. "He seems to have tumbled hard."

"Very flattering."

"I'm not saying that to enhance your ego."

"I think I will take a dip," Marion said and stood up.

"The water can wait a little longer."

"You always want to push your brother."

As they talked, they were suddenly dusted with sand and sprayed with droplets of water by a group of little girls running from the ocean to their blankets. Sandra used her towel to wipe off the sand. "My family means a lot to me," she said.

You don't show it with Neil or Toby, Marion wanted to tell her. If you gave them half the attention you devote to Eddie, maybe Neil wouldn't look elsewhere.

Sandra filled her cupped hand with sand, then idly let it dribble through her fingers. "Eddie is serious about you."

"We only met a few weeks ago."

"What difference does that make? The first time I met Neil I knew I wanted to marry him."

"Neil is special," Marion risked.

"The packaging is exceptional," Sandra said in her dry way.

"This discussion doesn't sound like you." She must know, Marion thought.

"What do you mean?"

"For a clever girl, you're going about the whole thing the wrong way. This idea of a heart-to-heart talk and pushing your brother. Don't you see how silly it is? Falling in love doesn't work according to plan." Without waiting for Sandra to protest, Marion stepped over someone's lunchbox and headed for the ocean.

The water felt a little warmer after a while, and Marion floated, letting the waves lift her and set her down in lulling rhythm. Her mind refused to cope with problems and she let herself relax. It was easy to gauge where the water became too deep merely by watching the furthest line of swimmers. Beyond them, only a few hardy souls dared to swim. Marion tried to decide whether the lifeguards on their white lookout posts watched the ones out there, who were probably the strongest swimmers, or if they concentrated on cowards like her, who would never venture into deep water. Now there was a thought, to try the classic gambit and attract a lifeguard like a giddy teenager. She floated on her back and glanced quickly at the nearest lifeguard post, but it was hard to tell the age of the muscular figure atop it. Maybe she should come out to Bay Two alone one of these days and be picked up. If you had never done the wild things in high school or college, they were still in your system. Marion knew she would soon reach the point where nothing could be worse than remaining alone.

She let a wave carry her closer to the beach and tried to detect Sandra in the crowd, but saw at least half a dozen beach chairs like theirs. Before she left the water, Marion thought, she must figure out what to say if Sandra suspected her attraction for Neil.

When Marion did come out of the water though, Sandra was buying a popsicle for Toby.

"This is about the only place where he can eat chocolate ice cream without utter disaster."

Marion laughed because it seemed necessary but she couldn't talk to Toby the way expected of adults. She should say, "That looks delicious" or "I wish your mommy had gotten one for me," but he intimidated her.

"Go and play," Sandra told her son and flopped neatly onto her chair.

"We shouldn't stay too long; it's early in the season."

"I figure about another hour." Sandra started to reapply suntan lotion on her shoulders. "I'm serious about talking to you, so don't run away again."

"I came to the beach so I went into the water. That's not running away."

"I don't care to see my brother hurt."

"After two dates."

"He's a very intense guy, and he's been hurt before."

"What do you want from me, Sandra? I didn't even care to go out with him."

"But now you're seeing him steadily."

"That's not from choice. He won't listen to reason when I try to refuse a date."

"Neil says people with strong personalities can be disliked. Part of the pattern. Is that the problem with my brother?"

"Because I'm alone and susceptible, my friends needn't dig up men for me. Believe me, I don't like living alone. If you want to know the truth, I'm absolutely miserable, but I can find my own men."

"Here," Sandra offered. "Take some of this lotion before you burn."

"My skin's darker than yours."

"I think it's time to stop worrying about you altogether."

"That suits me. I don't need help."

"Fine."

"And you can tell your brother to leave me alone, too."

"I'll do that little thing."

"Don't be so snooty about it, Sandra. I'm not exactly an old maid, you know. Anyone can lose a husband."

Sandra didn't answer. She rolled over onto her stomach and fished a book out of her straw bag.

Now I understand why women sometimes pull each other's hair or scratch each other's eyes out, Marion thought. When the shoe is on the other foot, she'll be sorry she patronized me. "You've acted superior for a long time."

"I tried to stand by and be there when you needed me."

"You enjoyed helping 'poor Marion,' isn't that it?"

"Do you realize the state you were in when Alec was killed?"

"I never asked for any favors."

"For God's sake, Marion, what's the matter with you today? You were recovering from a blow that would level anyone and you had the additional burden of loving the person you blame for the disaster."

"I don't want to hear about that."

"Whenever I mention your mother, you panic."

"Leave Mama out of this," Marion said so shrilly that two older ladies on the blanket in front of them turned to stare at her.

"You need a good psychiatrist."

"You think you know it all but one of these days..." Marion folded her aluminum chair, threw everything into her carryall and stalked away, trying for a dignified departure, impeded as it was every step of the way by the masses of people on the beach, but vowing to herself she would show Sandra she needed no pity.

Fotolia #42734875 street sign, Brooklyn © alb470

Many years later, Marion discovered Roz had said nothing further about the betting pool because she'd trusted her cousin would not break up the Kramer marriage.

Chapter 12

A s the June days grew longer, the Mediterranean's playground swarmed with children running between swings and seesaws. Many of the parents were nowhere in sight, but the sandbox had a sprinkling of toddlers whose mothers occasionally shouted at them not to eat sand. Roz knew few of these women by name, although she'd often noticed them in the elevators or in the lobby. They seemed to have separated into small cliques based on the ages of their children. One day, she would sit here rocking a carriage, Roz promised herself, and be just like the others. Now, as she walked past the park loaded with packages from the supermarket, Harriet called to her.

"What's your hurry?"

"These packages are heavy."

"Why don't you go to that place on the next corner? They deliver. Boy, I can tell you, I never carry anything."

Roz didn't want to say that she saved money this way. "There is more choice at the supermarket."

"So you have everything sent from the grocery and what they don't have, you pick up at the supermarket. Still less to carry that way." Harriet showed with a certain upward tilt of head that she saw through Roz's excuse and that such considerations were not part of her own life.

Roz wanted to get the perishables into her refrigerator, but she was afraid to offend the other woman by rushing off. Harriet made no move toward continuing their conversation and Roz, knowing she should say something breezy and move on, found herself rooted to the playground area.

Harriet fanned herself with a magazine. She was perspiring heavily and seemed unable to get comfortable. "Interesting things happen in summertime. The humidity does it."

"But all here have the air-conditioned apartments."

"It's in the air. A sultriness. Why do you think so many couples get married in June?"

"Is that not the custom?"

"Oh, you know what I mean."

"My English is not yet..."

Harriet shrugged as if to say "You wouldn't try to kid me, would you?" and abruptly reminded Roz of the girl who'd tormented her when she'd first arrived in Florida from Cuba. Sue Ellen's eyes had narrowed into the same little slits when she wanted something from Roz. As a life-long resident of Miami, Sue Ellen hated the tourists but, at least, as she told Roz Geller during Roz's first day in an American high school, the tourists brought in money while the refugees just waited to get on relief.

"I hate them all," Sue Ellen said.

After that brief, bitter introduction, Sue Ellen appointed herself Roz's sponsor at school. She helped Roz with her English, explained things to her and was Roz's only friend. But Sue Ellen was impatient.

"I told you a million times," she would say, "don't get that stupid look on your face when you can't understand. Act smart and people will think you're smart. I'm tired of being ashamed of you."

"I will be carefully."

"Careful."

"I will be careful."

"Just oil your brain and remember."

"The composition that we must write, have you finished it, Sue Ellen?"

"Mine's done, but you can't copy it."

"I do not want to copy."

"Okay, so write your own composition, and I'll tell you what's wrong and you can do it over."

"Okay."

Sue Ellen smiled. "Now you sound American. Soon, I'll be able to recommend you to my uncle for that job."

"The job, it is very important for me."

"Don't worry about a thing, kid. It's practically set."

It was good to hear Sue Ellen confirm her pledge. Roz had assured her mother and father that her new North American friend had connections and despite fierce competition from other new arrivals, Roz would soon be working.

"When will you know for certain?"

"Pretty soon. Say, Roz, can you carry this for a while?" Sue Ellen handed Roz her stack of textbooks.

Not daring to ask further questions, Roz walked along silently, loaded down with her own and the other girl's books.

At the corner where their paths diverged, Roz returned the books. She had carried them to this corner for Sue Ellen every afternoon for the past month.

"Some of you Cubans must have escaped with money or diamonds or something like that. You can't all be poor."

"I do not know." Roz bit the cuticle of her thumb and waited to hear what Sue Ellen wanted now.

"And I've seen some real handsome fellows."

"Yes."

"Why don't you introduce me to one?" Sue Ellen asked. "But not from a welfare family."

Of all the small favors Roz had been called upon to perform for Sue Ellen, this seemed the most impossible, but it would be necessary just as it was necessary to carry her books and packages. Roz would have to find a way.

For a few weeks, despising herself all the time, she played Sue Ellen's game and stalled, but Sue Ellen finally came through with the job and Roz began work as a waitress. The demands and condescension of the other girl now increased but Roz no longer had time after school and Sue Ellen gradually dropped her. At first, Roz lived in terror that the job would be withdrawn but she managed to hold onto it.

Now, Harriet leaned forward to whisper to Roz and her resemblance to the girl from Florida evaporated. "They need to be shoved," Harriet said.

As in the old days with Sue Ellen, Roz wanted to avoid anger, so she looked attentive and waited to discover what her neighbor was talking about.

"I'm determined to win the pool." She pointed a pudgy finger at Roz.

"Please, can you not stop it?"

"Are you kidding? I picked June."

June—the month had just begun, but perhaps if the entire month went by uneventfully, Harriet would change her mind.

"I thought you are the friend of Sandra."

"Friend, my eye. She's had it too good for too long. Always asking me so sweetly, 'Is Shelley out of town again?' As if I didn't know what the women say behind my back."

"I have never heard anyone talk about you. Really, Harriet."

"My Shelley wouldn't look at another woman. And your cousin is the worst one. She used to brag that her husband never went anywhere without her, as if she didn't know mine has to travel for his job."

"My cousin would do nothing wrong," Roz said, the words bitter in her mouth.

"A lot you know about life."

Roz started to lift her packages and escape.

"The first chance Marion gets to latch onto a dreamboat like Neil Kramer, she'll use the opportunity, I guarantee it. Now all I have to do is make it a little easier for them before the month is over."

"Only to win the money of this pool?"

"Listen, I have all the money I need. My apartment is the biggest available in this building, we have a terrace, and we take the garage. Every week when Shelley gets paid, he hands me the whole thing and says to go out and buy myself something nice." Harriet suddenly jumped up and yelled at her little boy not to throw sand around.

"Then why do you want to win?"

"All the girls expect me to be the winner."

Roz chose her words carefully so Harriet would not fly into a Sue Ellen type rage. "I would not like to break up a home."

"Sandra has better than she deserves. I don't feel a bit sorry for her, the stuck-up thing."

Harriet's little boy ran over to them and threw his pail at his mother. "What do you think you're doing? I'll split your head for you."

"Push, push."

"He wants to go on the swings."

It was a good chance to escape and Roz started to leave but Harriet ran back and caught her at the gate to the playground. "Wait a minute."

Why should I obey her, Roz asked herself. There is no job dependent on her favor, and she can do nothing worse than ignore me from now on. But the habit of listening was too ingrained in Roz and she worried that Harriet, with her vicious tongue, would turn the other neighbors against her. When you were tied to an apartment with a three-year lease, you could not afford to make enemies in the building.

After a while, Harriet returned to the gateway. "Have some of this. It's imported chocolate."

"Thank you."

"What I'm going to do, I got it all figured out. This Saturday, if I can get Sandra and Toby away for a few hours, Neil will be home alone. All that's left is to make sure that Marion knows it."

"But it is cruel to throw them together deliberately."

"Nature will take care of the matter for me or Marion's false eyelashes will."

"My cousin is very lonely. Why must you tempt her?"

"I'm helping her out."

"Neil is not for her."

"What are you talking about? She gets the best part of the deal. Everyone flips over Neil."

"He is nothing," Roz said, but in the face of Harriet's insistence, wondered whether she was mistaken.

"If I didn't have Shelley, I'd go for Neil myself."

"You will ruin my cousin's life."

"Girls don't get ruined that way anymore. Besides, if anyone can take care of herself, it's Marion. Look how quickly she got over her husband's death."

"That is not true," Roz said.

"I don't care what you say. My mind's made up." Harriet took her son by the arm and put him into his stroller.

"I will have to warn Marion."

"Tough," Harriet said and left the playground.

Roz went back through the gate and sat on one of the gold-and-white benches for a long time, oblivious to the fact that some of her groceries needed refrigeration. It was all right to defend Marion and threaten to warn her, but Marion had told Roz to mind her own business, making her helpless to stop Harriet.

After a while, Roz entered the building and took the elevator to her apartment. When she saw Sandra's door across the hall, a new idea came to her, to tell Sandra about Harriet's plans, but she soon realized this would worsen matters for her cousin.

Why am I so certain Marion will run to Neil? Roz asked herself. I know that she is attracted to him, but Marion will surely not begin an affair. She wants a husband.

Roz, suddenly exhausted, unpacked the last two cans of tuna fish, folded the bag, and went into the bedroom to rest before preparing dinner. Marty would tell her what to do, she thought, but before he came home, Roz remembered her husband's insistence that they were not to become involved. She couldn't act; she could only trust Marion.

Marion had enjoyed Eddie's company—and not merely because she was so lonely—she admitted now. Eddie was intelligent, he made her laugh, and he seemed to understand her. Would she have fallen in love with him if not dazzled by Neil? Even 40 years later, Marion couldn't find an answer to that question.

Chapter 13

The empty weekend stretched ahead of Marion, harder to endure after spending the past two Saturdays with Eddie. Although he didn't excite her the way Neil did, Eddie was company of sorts and she found she missed him.

Marion walked about the apartment, circling the living room, pausing now and then to look out the windows. She could see only traffic. Yesterday, she had visited Mama and Aunt Lena during the morning, setting aside the afternoon for an appointment at the beauty salon where she decided to have a manicure as well as a shampoo and set. At night, she watched television and so Friday had passed. But with nothing to look forward to on Saturday evening, time oppressed her.

Tapping one silver-enameled forefinger against her chin, Marion surveyed the living room, hoping to find some bit of cleaning to occupy her time, but everything was in place, the furniture dusted and polished, the carpet vacuumed.

She could ring down to the renting-agent's office and have Mr. Fontanna send up his son Joey to wash her windows but she didn't really like to talk to Joey, the smart aleck. Better to have the windows done while she was out shopping and not give him the idea she wanted to socialize with him.

Marion looked out the window again. After a time, she remembered she'd saved the dry cleaning for today and wandered into the bedroom to busy herself in the closet, picking out whatever needed pressing. This job ended quickly, but Marion forced herself to postpone grabbing the clothes and hurrying to the cleaners until afternoon. Her days were full of little tricks like that. Two months ago, she had let go the girl who'd come in one day a week to clean. She avoided broadcasting to the other women in the building that she did her own housework now, but Marion was glad she'd thought of the idea. Dividing the apartment into five sections, she managed to spend an hour to an hour-and-a-half most mornings doing the work the girl had done.

Marion picked up a Redbook that had come in the mail a few days ago, but books and magazines held her attention only for short spells; she couldn't concentrate on even the lightest of fiction. She turned on the television set. This is how I was right after Alec died, Marion thought, but then I didn't really want to be lifted out of the fog. It was like an anesthetic. Since she'd started going out again, the fog had dissipated and she could no longer isolate herself.

These aimless days would be over if I encouraged Eddie, Marion told herself, but there'd be little excitement in marriage with Eddie. If only Neil were free or if he were willing to divorce Sandra and marry me. What a terrible fight with Mama that would cause. It would be worth it, though. Anything was better than continuing this way.

Marion slumped down in the white velvet chair across the room from her television set and fiddled with the remote until only an hour remained before lunch, but she cheated and slowly ate a pastrami sandwich ahead of time. Now she would go downstairs and stroll to the dry cleaning shop, taking time to look in store windows along the way.

The Mediterranean Arms playground that Marion stared into hopefully as she passed by, was empty. She ambled along, torn between her desire to make the errand last as long as possible and her unwillingness to appear without purpose if a neighbor caught sight of her.

Three people ahead of her at the cleaners, a short conversation with the girl who waited on her, a slow walk back to the Arms, and then there was nothing left but to return to her empty apartment. Marion lingered in the lobby, reluctant to face the long afternoon.

"Haven't seen much of you now that you have a boyfriend," Harriet said, appearing near the elevator.

Marion had a distinct urge to punch her stout neighbor but smiled at her instead. "How are you doing?"

"Not too badly. The children are driving me crazy, but I'm going to take them to the new Disney movie later. Sandra is bringing Toby."

"I've never been able to sit through a children's show."

"Exactly what our husbands said, so we gals are stuck. Well, you lucky thing, no one can force you to go."

Harriet's satisfied expression made Marion strongly doubt she was unhappy about the movie. "You can always shut your eyes," she said.

"From one o'clock until after five o'clock? That's a long catnap with hundreds of children howling around us."

"It's television for me. Better for napping."

"Have fun," Harriet said and stepped across the lobby into the mailroom.

I wonder what that was all about, Marion thought. She seemed to be lying in wait for me. Probably just watching for the mail.

Marion waited for the elevator, took it up to the third floor, and paced slowly down the long corridor to her apartment. The idea of spending the rest of the afternoon and evening in front of the television suddenly seemed impossible, but it wasn't until Marion had frantically pushed the button from channel to channel that she realized what Harriet's words meant. Neil would be alone all afternoon. She had not seen him after the night he'd answered her call for company. At least a dozen times since then, Marion considered telephoning to say she was frightened again, but it was more likely Sandra would answer the summons. And Neil, if he responded, would expect to spend the night.

Well, why not, Marion asked herself. All my life, I abided by religious and moral conventions and where did it get me? Less than three years after we married, Alec was dead, our life together cut short as though we deserved punishment for some unknown transgression. Would it do any good to deny herself happiness when it could so quickly be snatched away? Mama and I don't live under the same roof any more. There's no one to watch, no one to know what I do.

For a good part of the afternoon, Marion daydreamed about Neil. Several times, she started to leave for his apartment only to halt midway. She bathed, lingering in the tub, considering whether she dared go to him and hated herself for hesitating. They wanted each other. No other woman would waste time debating the question as though it were a world crisis. She wondered whether she'd deliberately quarreled with Sandra at the beach to overcome her sense of loyalty and friendship. If you spend the rest of your life alone when you have this chance to change things, Marion told herself, you deserve to be unhappy.

After her long bath, she changed to a black eyelet dress and, stockingless, but with high-heeled pumps, carefully made up her face and brushed her hair. She pretended to herself that she was still uncommitted, but her decision had been made the moment she questioned adherence to Mama's code. Nothing worse could happen to her than what she'd already experienced.

Marion walked up the seldom used staircase of the Mediterranean Arms to avoid meeting any neighbors in the elevator. At the first ring of the bell, Neil threw open the door as though he'd expected her. She had, before coming to the apartment, decided to pretend a message for Sandra, feigning ignorance of the fact that Neil's wife was not at home. He made it easy, chewing on his pipe and taking her presence naturally. He offered her something cool to drink and Marion automatically pulled the door chain across the inside of the apartment door as she followed Neil into the living room, amused at herself for worrying about burglars now.

"Have you been hiding from me?" Neil asked.

"Should I be?" Marion bit her lip, annoyed at the coy words.

"I've been here all afternoon, lonely as hell, when we could have entertained each other." Neil set two glasses on the starkly modern coffee table and settled Marion on the sofa before joining her.

"I know all about loneliness, but one afternoon isn't much."

"It can be."

They might continue to spar this way or he could renew his suggestion of the other evening. Now that Marion had made up her mind, Neil seemed to have no intention of making love to her.

"I always enjoy being with you," Marion said and smiled at him.

Neil put down his pipe and put his arm around her, drawing her closer, tightening the embrace when she responded to it. Neil's kiss evoked excitement that frightened Marion. Her need for him made her shiver in anticipation and Neil seemed to sense this at once. In a few minutes, maneuvering until Marion was full length on the sofa, Neil removed first her dress, then his own clothing with one hand while he caressed her with the other. Marion helped him take off her black lacy bra and matching lace panties. Wanting to be closer to his warm body, she arched her own upwards, which Neil took as a signal that she was ready for him. After one brief moment when she almost screamed Alec's name instead of Neil's, Marion stopped thinking.

"I've always wanted you," Neil whispered.

Marion didn't want to talk and come down to earth again but suddenly through the haze, she heard a key turn in the door at the other end of the living room and a metallic snap as the door chain pulled taut.

"Now I've got you," Sandra said, her voice loud and nearly hysterical.

Neil jumped off the sofa, pulled on his shorts and stood in the doorway trying to calm Sandra, without releasing the door chain to allow her into the apartment and Marion realized he was giving her time. She ducked behind the sofa to dress. It wasn't until she emerged, knowing the moment could no longer be postponed, that Marion became aware of three women staring at her through the partially opened door.

Fotolia #32107417 - Grand Army Plaza in Prospect Park, Brooklyn © SeanPavonePhoto

Marion wanted to restart the ignition and pull away from the Mediterranean Arms but knew she wasn't ready. Even 40 years after that day, she couldn't relive it without remembering exhilaration followed by mortification. She remembered, too, how Neil fled the apartment, leaving her to face Sandra and the possibility of eviction from the building on moral grounds. Her humiliation had been complete despite her show of defiance.

Chapter 14

Y ou can damn well get yourself a divorce."

"I sure as hell will," Neil said.

"And open this door right now."

Neil complied with his wife's order, speeding from the apartment as she rushed in. Marion watched him go and bit her lip to avoid begging him not to leave her.

When the door was thrown wide, Marion saw that Roz and Harriet were the two women with Sandra. Her mind blank, she ran past them trying for a quick escape to her own apartment, but Sandra barred the way.

"Where are you going?"

"Home."

"Go ahead, run away," Harriet yelled, sounding as though she had caught her own husband with Marion.

Marion hesitated, not knowing whether to push through or wait. She noticed Roz was crying.

"So it was my husband you wanted all along," Sandra's voice was strangely harsh.

"You patronized me all these months—now you know what it's like to lose a husband."

"I was drawn to you; I wanted to help."

"No selfish reasons? It didn't give you a lift to be nice to poor Marion?"

"I did have another reason but you wouldn't believe it." Sandra looked away. "Guilt because of the times I had imagined Neil dead, wished for it, speculated how my life would be without him."

"You're right! I don't believe you."

Sandra shrugged. "It's fashionable to blame the victim, anyhow. 'No, it wasn't little Johnny's fault. He stole that car because the man didn't lock it up.'" Sandra's voice became harsher. "Of course, it's not your fault, Marion. I guess I didn't use the right deodorant or hairspray or something equally important."

"Don't, Sandra." Marion's defiance crumbled and her initial shame and humiliation returned. "It just happened. We love each other."

"Love my eye," Harriet said.

"Did you have to use my apartment?"

"Your husband, your apartment. It follows."

"That's enough, Harriet. I can handle my own affairs."

"You mean your husband's affairs, don't you?" Harriet's eyes narrowed, emphasizing their hooded, lizard-like appearance.

"One of the children is crying," Roz interrupted, forcing Harriet to run across the hall and check.

"What do you intend to do now?" Sandra asked Marion.

"I don't know."

"As far as I'm concerned, Neil can get out today and take a plane to Reno or the Virgin Islands or wherever you get an easy divorce these days. You can have him and good luck. But I'll never forgive you for the way you repaid my friendship."

"I told you it wasn't planned."

"Wasn't it? Do you wear black lace panties every day in the week?"

Marion tried to leave again, but this time Harriet's return blocked her.

"The kids were fighting over a toy, same as you girls," she said sarcastically.

Harriet turned to Roz. "A living room without furniture like yours is a good place for them to play," she said.

Roz paid no attention, staring at Marion until her cousin became aware of it. "Grow up, Roz. This is the real world."

"Do you mean only children are innocent? If you were not ashamed, you would not make excuses."

"What's the matter, ladies? Another robbery?" Mr. Fontanna appeared in the doorway. Marion had no idea how much he'd heard.

"No, no, it's nothing." Sandra said.

"Someone called down on the intercom to say there was a disturbance in 5G."

"We're just talking." Marion forced herself to speak calmly.

"Now ladies, this is the Arms. We can't have disturbances."

"If it's so elegant here, why do you rent to tramps?"

Marion heard Harriet in horror, realizing for the first time that the consequences would outweigh her momentary embarrassment. She had read about people found in compromising positions often enough for the phrase to become a newspaper cliché, but now it had happened to her. Until this moment, it seemed as though she'd been watching a stranger's life unreel instead of her own. If they'd seen me on the toilet, I would have felt more awkward, she told herself. This way, humiliation was tinged with a certain sense of triumph because she'd succeeded in getting Neil and this, in turn, might free him from his marriage.

"When we heard Mrs. Kramer scream, we thought it was a burglar," Harriet was saying. "We were all in 5R across the hall, and she went to get something to show me." The stout girl was perspiring and stopped to wipe her forehead with a tissue.

"This is personal, Mr. Fontanna," Sandra said with dignity. "We'll call you if there's any need."

"All good and well, ladies, but I have to do my job. If any story spreads around to spoil the reputation of the Arms, I'm responsible." He spoke as though the building were an old and valued friend.

"Then throw her out." Harriet pointed to Marion.

"Mrs. Davis has a lease, same as you."

"I don't need immoral neighbors."

"Why don't you go to your own apartment, Harriet?" Sandra said. "I'm very tired."

"You ought to back me up."

"Why do you hate me?" Marion asked Harriet.

"Ladies, ladies. Calm down. We'll be getting complaints from all the apartments on this floor."

"You should have come sooner. Then you'd have seen that animal doing it right in front of everyone."

Roz gasped and Marion turned away from her.

"There is a clause in the lease about moral turpitude," said Mr. Fontanna in the same dry voice he always used.

"Then get rid of her," Harriet said.

"And she'll forfeit the two month's rent she paid for security."

He sounded so smug, Marion wanted to smash something. Why were they judging her when none of them had suffered as she had? Was it so unusual for one human to turn towards another because of overwhelming loneliness?

"We want to avoid a fuss, Mr. Fontanna," Sandra said. "And I'm sure the building doesn't want a scandal either."

"If you force my cousin to move, we will also leave," Roz told him.

"Personally, I saw nothing. But if any tenant files a formal complaint by registered letter, I'll have to take the matter up with the landlord."

"That won't be necessary." Sandra looked frostily at Harriet. "Everyone will mind her own business."

Marion was grateful to be spared the final degradation of eviction from the Mediterranean Arms. She did not want to live with Neil in the apartment she'd shared with Alec but to be forced out of the building was another matter. After a while, if she married Neil, people would forget today.

"You're a coward," Harriet said to Sandra. "No wonder she took your husband so easily."

"She can have him."

"Women like you spoil it for everyone else."

"This isn't a circus. Let's have a little dignity."

"If you ladies have any further difficulty, call my office." Mr. Fontanna hurriedly left the apartment.

Sandra walked across the room, avoiding the sofa and sat on one of her Danish chairs, leaning forward with her head in her hands. "Neil never had any sense," she said.

"Make up your mind. First you don't want him; then you do."

"Don't worry, we'll be divorced. Unfortunately, I was unprepared and neglected to take pictures, so Neil will have to travel for the divorce and then he's all yours. You can enjoy living the great marriage myth."

"But how can one be happy at the expense of another?" Roz asked.

"Neil couldn't have been very content with you, Sandra."

"That's the usual alibi."

"We need each other."

"You're getting what you deserve; that is, if he is willing to marry you. Did he promise marriage?"

"We didn't talk about that."

"You really lost your head, didn't you? You poor fool."

Marion, furious at being patronized again, decided Sandra wanted to discourage her and keep her away from Neil, but she vowed nothing would prevent them from being together now.

Fotolia #30880359 Manhattan Bridge at sunset, New York City © EastVillageImages

Before Marion could forgive Roz, she'd had to forgive herself. The cousins never did become close, but eventually they talked about the day that changed Marion's life. A terrible day, but she saw it in perspective now. It couldn't compare with the one in which Alec had died.

Chapter 15

When Marion left the Kramer apartment, Roz needed to go too, but she wanted to avoid Harriet. Her cousin's disgrace had made Roz sick, her stomach queasy with the knowledge that she should have warned Marion. She vowed to be courageous from now on. No one would intimidate her again.

Only a little while ago, Harriet had taken the elevator upstairs to the fifth floor with Sandra on the pretext of seeing the Geller's bedroom set. Roz quickly invited both of them in and tried to keep them in her apartment but after a few minutes, Harriet managed to send Sandra across the hall to get toys for Toby, Phyllis, and Phyllis' baby brother. Certain Marion had resisted the bait, Roz nevertheless thought of telephoning her cousin but before she could act, Marion and Neil were exposed. I must not reveal I knew about Harriet's plot, Roz decided as she felt Sandra's contempt for Harriet and herself.

"Why did you orchestrate it?" Sandra asked Harriet.

"How can you blame me?"

"You orchestrated it."

"What am I, a marriage broker?"

"They were sitting ducks for your viciousness, weren't they?"

Harriet looked at her and smiled. "You had it coming. All of you sneer because my Shelley is always out-of-town. But it wasn't Shelley playing around—it was your marvelous husband, the dreamboat of the whole building."

"Look closely someday."

Sandra turned towards Roz. "And what satisfaction did you get out of this?"

Roz crushed a tissue in her hand and stood there, knowing how stupid she must seem. "I was not a part of it."

"You didn't know."

"I knew but I could not stop Harriet."

"And you never tried to warn me to stay home today."

There was no possible answer, Roz thought. She'd been sure her cousin wouldn't fall into the trap, but anything said now would make matters worse. She'd worried about her cousin, not Sandra, and yet it was Sandra who suffered. In Neil's wife now, she saw a slight ambivalence as though she were undecided whether to be more upset over finding her husband with Marion or the manipulation that led to it.

The scene had been staged, whether the two principals knew it or not, and Roz—even though she'd experienced malevolence disguised as friendship in Miami—was unable to believe Harriet could be so cruel. "Is it not better to know of what people are capable?" she asked Sandra.

"No, it's better to have illusions."

"Even when you see through them?"

"Now the dream will be Marion's and it will be a long time before she sees what it is."

"This pretense is not life," Roz said. "You Americans no longer know the difference."

"You don't even care," Harriet told Sandra. "No wonder Neil turned to another woman."

"Would it satisfy you to know I do care? Or do you feel less evil this way?"

"Don't take it out on me."

"You're much worse than Marion."

Roz saw the hatred build in Harriet's lizard-like face and tried to forestall further argument. "We must see what the children are doing."

"You don't give a damn about Toby," Harriet told Sandra, "but I care about my children." She ran into Roz's apartment, took Phyllis and her little boy, and dragged them away.

Toby was crying and Sandra went to get him. Although he still sobbed when Sandra brought him back to her own apartment, Roz saw that his mother made no attempt to comfort him.

"You've met Roberta," Sandra said to Roz. "When she first moved into this building, she was quite different, very sweet in fact, until she came under Harriet's influence. It's happening to you. You're on the sidelines now when Harriet's tongue dissects everyone, but soon you'll make a tentative stab at character assassination to gain her approval. After a while you'll vie with her in cutting remarks."

"No, no. I have learned." Roz crossed over to her own apartment and started to straighten it out. Several magazines were shredded on the living room floor, but Harriet had been right. Children couldn't do much damage when she had so little furniture. She made quick work of the mess, her mind still on the afternoon's scene. When Roz and Harriet ran to the doorway of the Kramer's apartment at Sandra's shout, they'd seen only that Marion and Neil were nude, but Roz surmised Neil's wife had caught them in the act. She tried to imagine herself discovered that way, but the idea was too repugnant. Yet Marion appeared triumphant rather than ashamed.

When Marty came home from his office, Roz found herself telling him at once, although she had cautioned herself to wait.

"That's savoir-faire," Marty said.

"You cannot be laughing."

"It's just the punchline of an old joke. I couldn't resist saying it."

"You have asked me not to become involved, Marty, and I have tried, but I am entangled with all of them."

"Who was it claimed New Yorkers never know their neighbors?"

"You are in a strange mood, treating this as a joke."

"What do you want me to do? So she slept with him. Maybe he'll want to marry her; maybe he won't."

"Please do not be cruel, Marty. I have seen too much cruelty today."

"Listen, your cousin is getting enough excitement to last her a lifetime. Maybe, a little embarrassment is mixed in, but I'll bet she feels like Cleopatra. And she isn't mooning around for a dead man anymore."

"What will Cousin Bertha do?"

"Marion's mother doesn't enter into the picture. She'll be horrified that her daughter's taken up husband-snatching, but Marion will either marry Neil and Bertha'll forget how she acquired her new son-in-law or Marion will get worse and this will have been a minor incident."

"You do not understand. People from the old country are not so worldly. Had I acted in this way, it would have killed my mother."

"Roz, all of them are over twenty-one. They're not going to take advice from us. Very few lonely women would withstand Neil; they don't see any further than his handsome profile."

"Why does she have so much hurry?"

"That's easy."

"And now she has lost the brother of Sandra most certainly." Roz stared ahead for a few moments, trying to think of something she could do to atone for standing by this afternoon. "You must have a friend we can introduce to Marion."

"Are you serious? I believe that's just what your cousin fights against—everyone trying to palm off favorite bachelors and she's supposed to be grateful."

"No, I mean it. Maybe it is not too late."

"This isn't the way to go about helping Marion."

"It is a beginning. For the first time in my life, I will act and not stand stupidly on the sidelines."

Marty reached into his pocket and took out a small address book. "Anyone I know well enough to greet with more than 'lousy weather today' is in this book." He handed it to Roz.

Flipping carefully through the pages of the address book, Roz found several names she didn't recognize and Marty admitted one of the men was unmarried and not too repulsive.

"Would he call Marion if you give him the telephone number?"

"This is ridiculous."

"Please, Marty. I am to blame for what happened this afternoon."

"You're wrong, but I'll do it for you. I'll let him know she's a damn pretty girl."

Roz looked at her husband, the old worry that he would become interested in one of the self-confident American girls stabbing her. Would Marty have resisted if her cousin had chosen this apartment instead of Neil's?

"Stop frowning. I'm not interested in our local siren."

"She is so charming and so sophisticated. I can never learn to be like her."

"Who wants you to be like the women in this building?"

"I will ask Marion tomorrow if your friend may call her." Marty started to protest again, she noticed, but changed his mind. Instead, he pocketed the address book and stood up.

"Please don't tell your friend about Neil."

"He isn't the one you have to worry about. Your cousin won't want her number handed out like she's desperate for a fellow."

But Roz had resolved to help Marion smooth out the mess she was making of her life; whether she succeeded or failed, she must take the first step.

Fotolia #57837082 - Subway Stop Downtown & Brooklyn New York City © anujakjaimook

Had she really loved Neil or had she been drawn to him only because of overwhelming loneliness? She'd lived at home until marriage, as most young women did in those days, and Marion had never been on her own until Alec's death.

Chapter 16

Saturday night, Marion couldn't sleep at all and on Sunday she found herself unable and unwilling to get out of bed. She didn't relive the moments with Neil making love to her while Sandra tried to unlock the door. Marion had been through another kind of hell when Alec died so needlessly, and nothing could be as bad again. She considered the future instead. There was no reason now for Neil to gradually approach his wife for a divorce, and Marion was relieved to find events moving her way at last. If flouting all she'd been taught caused temporary humiliation and guilt, and if she must suffer now for future happiness, Marion was willing to pay the price.

In this frame of mind, she forgot about Eddie. When he arrived Sunday evening, she was wearing a white nylon housecoat.

"You look very virginal."

She had convinced herself that Sandra and Neil didn't really love each other. Eddie's tone made her realize for the first time how much her actions could hurt others. She was sorry, too, that Eddie would think less of her.

"I suppose you know," she said, pulling at a thread on her housecoat. "Then why did you come here?"

"To see you again."

"But it's useless."

"Do you have to marry every man you sleep with?"

Marion drew the housecoat more tightly around her. "Are you still trying to protect your sister?"

"No, I'm trying to protect you."

"Why?"

"I want to marry you."

He couldn't mean it, Marion knew. He was still trying to protect his sister, but something within her wished it were possible. How much easier life would be if she could accept his offer of escape.

"Neil won't appreciate you." Eddie said and moved forward to kiss her.

It was a nightmare. He held her too tightly and she could not free herself although it must have been clear to him she didn't respond to his embrace. This, then, was to be her punishment. If she had acquiesced once, she'd proven herself available.

"Am I that repulsive to you?" Eddie asked when he let her go.

"When you love someone, other men have no appeal."

"And right now, you're sure you love Neil?"

"Now and always."

Eddie laughed at her. "All of you see yourselves as teenagers, not women. Perpetual girls. How can you romanticize an itch for someone like Neil?"

Although Marion often did see herself as a "girl" rather than a grown woman, she wouldn't admit it to him. He was laughing, daring her to prove him wrong.

"What makes you think Neil will marry you?" Eddie continued.

"I don't know."

"My sister may not give him up so easily after all."

Marion pulled at the thread again. "He knows what I've been through. He wants me to be happy."

"You have a lot to learn, lamb. Either you grow through tragedy or you sink to a level where you'll eventually despise yourself."

"I'm pretty tired, Eddie. Please go."

"It has been a busy weekend for you at that. Eight months is a long time to remain celibate. I know all about it." His voice hardened. "But goddamn it, you could have waited."

"What do you know about it? All around me, in every other apartment, I knew people were loving each other. But there was no one for me anymore and never would be unless I took matters into my own hands." She shook her finger at him in her fury. "Condemn me. It will help your ego but if you want to understand, think of me alone for a couple of hundred nights and nothing to look forward to but more of the same."

"And what makes you think my situation is different?" Eddie asked. "I know you're lonely; I'm lonely, too.

"A man can always get someone to share his bed."

"Is that all you want Neil for?"

"Get out."

"No, I'm staying until we talk this over. I'm trying to find the answer to your madness."

For one brief moment, Marion wondered if he literally meant that she was insane, but that was impossible when he claimed to want to marry her. "There's no point in plaguing me."

"Marion, you're a lovely young woman. Don't throw your life away."

She was furious now. "Sandra sent you."

"My sister doesn't even know I'm here. If she did, she'd be angrier than you are. Don't be a fool!"

"What do you want from me?"

"I've told you—I want to help you."

"You're going to save me from myself, is that it?" Now she knew he would not miss the irony of her tone.

Eddie fingered the Havdalah box he had bought her that day in Connecticut and seemed to make up his mind. "Get dressed; we're going for a walk along the boardwalk.

"No."

"That's the least you can do for a rejected suitor. Don't worry; I'll wait out here for you."

"And will you leave after our walk?"

When he accepted her terms, she went into the bedroom and quickly put on a teal blue dress. The black eyelet one she'd worn yesterday was still on a chair and Marion hung it out of sight towards the back of her closet. Meanwhile, she planned what to say to Eddie. She was flattered that he wanted her despite the interlude with his brother-in-law or perhaps it enhanced her value in his eyes. No, that wasn't fair. Eddie had been interested in her before, and she should have let him down more easily. She wondered again if she could have fallen for Eddie, who seemed so decent, if she hadn't been dazzled by Neil. When they walked together, she'd try to be kind. Although she'd begun to live selfishly trying not to worry about the effect on anyone but herself, she could afford to be generous to Eddie.

The boardwalk was crowded, nearly every bench occupied although it was now close to eleven at night. Some of the knish and other snack places were open and many people walked along munching on "take out" food. The salty air revived Marion and made her forget that she'd barely slept the previous night.

Eddie walked along, saying nothing for a long time. It hurt her to realize he must be carefully weighing what to say, hunting desperately for a way to change her mind.

Sex appeal was a strange phenomenon. You met some men, and before they said a word, the magnetism was there. Here was someone who felt that way about Marion, but she was unable to care about him. He really was nice, and she tried to put herself in his shoes. Marion's only similar experience had been when she'd known her love for Alec well before he'd proposed, but she'd been aware Alec was attracted, too, that she had only to wait. It was all part of the excitement.

But Marion didn't want to think of Alec now or all Mama's talk about the hereafter would well up and she would start wondering if Alec could be aware of what she was doing.

God knows, Mama's another one I don't want on my mind, she thought.

As though Eddie could hear, he asked about Mama. "Was that your way of getting even?"

"She'll never find out. Why look for psychological reasons if I react physically to someone; affairs are commonplace now. That's today's world, not your idealized version."

"You didn't answer the question."

"Drop it, Eddie."

"Remember what I told you about the Emperor and his nightingale?"

"It has nothing to do with me."

"You've come to believe everyone acts only through self-interest because most of the people you meet are engaged in putting up a great front. Now you've joined them. But one day you'll want to go back to the genuine nightingale and find yourself left with a mechanical toy."

They were walking towards Brighton Third Street, and still hadn't passed any empty benches. Some had space for two more, but they both wanted privacy. After a while, Eddie led Marion to the railing and they looked down at the sand and across to the ocean. They could see the lights of the Rockaways in the distance and Marion wished she were far away, much further than those lights. She looked in the direction she believed must stretch out to Europe and could almost feel herself on an ocean liner heading for Le Havre— no problems, no one to worry about. Maybe she'd have a casual romance on board the ship. Nothing could be more glamorous. Marion sighed.

"It's not too late," Eddie said.

She looked at him, noticing again the crease in his chin when he smiled at her and wondering if he'd said something she'd missed.

Eddie took her hand and held it tightly. "One thing I promise you, there'll never be any mention of Neil between us. You don't need to have it on your mind."

"Other people know."

"Memories are short. Marion, you're dazzled by him now but give yourself time. We can have a good marriage and an exciting one, too."

She turned again towards the ocean.

"You think I'm dull."

Marion heard the sadness in his voice. "I do like you, but I can't give more. It's nothing personal."

"Thanks," he said drily.

"I'm flattered. You know that."

"Your ego doesn't need me."

"We should have met before."

"Would it have made any difference?" He started walking again, this time toward one of the stands that lined the boardwalk and bought each of them a hot dog. There was nothing more to say and Eddie seemed to realize it. As soon as they finished eating, they started again towards Sheepshead Bay and the Mediterranean Arms. The walk back was long and, once or twice, Eddie started to talk, beginning sentences he never finished.

Marion knew he felt sorry for her, but he was wrong; her life was just beginning again.

When Marion saw Mama for the last time, she never could have dreamed how much she'd miss her mother. Much she'd hated had translated into endearing quirks in her memory over the years.

Chapter 17

B efore the unveiling even, you are going to marry again?"
These were Bertha Benjamin's first words when Marion
finally brought herself to tell her mother and aunt that
she planned to marry Neil Kramer as soon as he returned from
Nevada.

"What does the unveiling have to do with it?"

"One year after a death comes the unveiling of the grave
marker. Jews like you who know nothing and care nothing
about religion are more destructive than a Hitler."

"Mama, I can't keep on living alone."

"You do not have faith enough to say 'God meant this to
be.'"

"For the rest of my life?"

"Not even a year and she wants to remarry," Bertha
Benjamin murmured half to herself. "And who's the great
metziah? Someone else's husband."

"Nobody worries about divorce these days."

"All the big shots on the television do it, so my daughter
must copy them. Someday, I wish you have a child to give
you back this aggravation."

"I'm old enough to make my own decisions."

"My neighbors, they come and ask me for advice, but
my daughter, she's too smart."

"Should I make some tea for us?" Marion asked, trying to change the subject.

"Make for your aunt, also."

"Where is Aunt Lena?" Marion had been counting on her aunt to help deflect Mama's reproaches.

"She went to buy a few things by the grocer."

"How come Aunt Lena does all the shopping?"

"We have our arrangement. Your aunt knows her job."

Marion figured Aunt Lena would rather be ordered about than argue. It seemed to her now that Aunt Lena had always done more than her share of the cooking, cleaning, and shopping for the household, another offense to chalk up against Mama, one she'd never noticed before.

Her mother settled heavily into a kitchen chair and watched every move as Marion started water boiling in the old teakettle, making her daughter nervous. Disapproval was etched into the lines around her mouth, startling Marion with the years they added to Mama's face. Since the stroke, Marion thought. How convenient it would be for her mother to have another stroke now, forcing me to visit the hospital daily, postponing marriage at least until her recovery.

"You work too hard, Mama." It was a reversal of what Marion had contemplated a few minutes ago, but she was barely aware of that.

"This apartment is not easy to keep up."

"Why don't you get a smaller one in a new building, everything fresh and clean, maybe a dishwasher?"

"For me a dishwasher is no good. I could not use it for both milchig and fleischig."

"You could use it for dairy and meat if you wanted."

Bertha Benjamin sighed. "If I don't observe the old laws, who will? You?"

The teakettle whistled and Marion deliberately turned her back and busied herself at the stove.

"A daughter should hate a mother, this they learn in America?"

"Mama, please. I must live my own life but that doesn't mean I hate anybody."

"And the in-laws in California, when they hear, what will they think?"

"Do they expect me to be an old maid?"

"An old maid, no. But the race to be married again this time? When you were in college and all your friends were showing diamond rings, you had to show a diamond ring, too."

"Neil and I are marrying as soon as he comes back."

"I am ashamed to tell anyone."

Marion felt like dashing the mismatched cups and saucers to the floor, but she put them neatly on the table instead. "You don't have to send out announcements this time."

"And a Rabbi, what Rabbi will marry you and this Neil?"

"Don't worry, it will be a Jewish ceremony."

"I cannot even think; you give me so much aggravation."

Marion exploded. "Don't you want me to be happy?"

"Maybe it would make you happy to steal a thousand dollars from the bank. Go ahead. God forbid I should keep you from being happy."

"Don't compare this with stealing. If Neil really loved Sandra, I couldn't take him away from her. He loves me, and only me and I didn't take anything that really belonged to anyone else."

"You know better than that. I brought you up and taught you right from wrong. I cannot stand this," Bertha Benjamin cried out.

"Mama, calm down."

"Do you have to get married? Is that why all the rush?"

Marion's hands grew cold despite the cup of hot tea she held. Although she was sure she wasn't pregnant, if Mama knew how she'd been caught with Neil in Sandra's apartment, her shrieks would be worse than anything before. No, she must lie. Mama hadn't believed her that time with Alec when she'd told the truth, but maybe that incident had tempered her judgment.

"Of course not," she said as strongly as she could.

"Thank God."

You're a liar and an adulterer, Marion told herself, and if Mama is right, you're a thief, too. But she didn't feel guilty the way she had when she'd hated Mama for causing the accident that killed Alec. The enormity of that hatred had seemed unbearable.

"Neil is coming back in three more weeks, and we're going to get married then."

"And you will all live happily ever after in the same apartment house."

"Sandra told him she'll move out."

"One of you at least has some sense."

"You may not agree, Mama, but we all are being very sensible about the whole thing."

"I wish I did not live to see this."

Marion was suddenly embarrassed as she decided how to phrase her next words. "You will see at the wedding that he is wonderful."

"I do not come to that wedding."

"Then Aunt Lena will see me through."

"Your aunt will not come either."

"You can't stop her. If you want to be small-minded, don't think Aunt Lena will agree with you."

"Neither of us comes to the wedding. Go ahead and get married, but remember you killed your mother."

"Stop it already, Mama."

"You'll find out."

Marion waited for her aunt, trying to avoid conversation with her mother, which was easy for Mama obviously had said her fill and now regarded her with tightly pressed lips. The expression was one Marion remembered, used so often during her adolescence that it had lost its effect.

Knowing she could depend on her aunt, Marion regained the sense of well-being she'd enjoyed since Neil came to see her the night before leaving for Reno. Until then, she hadn't been sure of him, but he said everything she'd dreamed of and left her looking forward to their wedding day.

When Aunt Lena walked in, she seemed neither surprised nor enthused to hear her niece had taken her advice to quickly remarry. She surveyed Marion as if she, too, wondered about a forced wedding. "You didn't waste much time."

Marion felt an intense desire to tell her aunt that she was the one who'd first heightened her awareness of Neil and her erotic feelings for him—but she restrained herself.

"We are not going to have anything to do with them," Mama shouted. "We are not going near them."

"Aunt Lena will come to my wedding."

"I will not allow it."

Aunt Lena looked down at her hands, but not before Marion saw embarrassment that at first she believed a result of Mama's outburst.

"You'll come, won't you?"

"Have you thought this over, Marion?"

"Of course, I have. I've thought about nothing else during the weeks Neil's been away getting his divorce. I write to him every day."

"And he writes to you every day."

"He has less time than I do."

"Why don't you get married quietly. It is, after all, a second wedding."

"It will be a quiet wedding, Aunt Lena, but someone from the family should be there. What will Neil's mother think?"

"Now you worry what she will think?" Mama yelled. "Better you should have thought about it before you sent her son for a divorce."

Marion nearly gave herself away, starting to say that Sandra had sent Neil for the divorce.

"Your mother doesn't want me at the wedding. I will do as she says."

"But why must you obey her? I don't understand this."

"Bertha has been good to me."

"Why will you desert me when I need you?" Marion felt herself near hysteria at the strangeness of her aunt's behavior.

"I'm sorry."

The fury that Marion felt again was directed against her mother. "You won't let me be happy. You begrudge it. First it was Alec. You hated him and you killed him. Now I have the chance to be happy with someone else, and you want to end my new life before it starts."

Aunt Lena ran to Mama who had clutched the edge of the kitchen sink for support and led her out of the room, one sister leaning heavily upon the other. With the knowledge that she'd said the unforgivable at last, Marion felt her guilt seep away. Now Mama would pretend to be ill, but Marion was through pretending. She'd stopped short of telling Mama she hated her but that, after all, was not true and Marion was adult enough to know it. In a few minutes, she would tell Aunt Lena she was glad it had all come into the open and that the air was cleared. From now on, after Mama got over the first shock of the marriage, their relationship would be a normal one. But when Aunt Lena returned to the kitchen, she would not say much to Marion, other than advising her to leave so Mama could rest.

It had taken Marion many years to forgive Roz for her cousin's careless revelation and even longer to admit she herself was the prime cause of the events that followed. Her cousin was trying to help, Marion learned later, but her attempt to make peace between Mama and Marion had backfired tragically.

Chapter 18

In August, discovering she was pregnant made Roz Geller want someone with whom to share her news. Her cousin Marion, who was married to Neil Kramer now and living in the same apartment she'd occupied before, was too indifferent toward Roz. For someone like Harriet or Bobbie to be told before her condition was obvious was distasteful, which left only Cousin Bertha. Roz hadn't visited her for some time and hoped Cousin Bertha would be pleased to see her.

She thought of inviting Marion to come along, but in the end went alone. Cousin Bertha seemed surprised. "My daughter sent you?"

"No, I do not see Marion very often."

"I do not see her at all; I have forgotten her." Bertha Benjamin folded her hands across her chest as if she dared Roz to contradict her. "And you, tell me, do you like it in that fancy building?"

"It is funny about the women there who have everything but spend their time counting up what everyone else has. Me, they leave alone. I think they have written me off as worthless."

"Do not worry about them."

"I'm too excited to think about those people. We are expecting a baby."

"Ah, your mother must be happy."

"We called them long distance."

"I have always wanted a grandchild."

Roz saw Cousin Bertha struggle with her own thoughts before she turned back to her and offered the inevitable cup of tea. While Cousin Bertha prepared the tea, Roz decided she must get Marion here somehow. Marion's mother seemed very unhappy.

"When is the baby due?"

"March." Roz could guess, though without being annoyed, that Cousin Bertha was counting the months since she and Marty married. All the old people did that automatically.

"Will your mother come up from Florida?"

"I do not know if Marty and I have the money to send her for fare."

"Maybe I can manage that."

"We have taken so much from you, Cousin Bertha."

"I am old and my sister Lena is getting old, too. There is enough to last us until the end."

She has always been so generous, Roz thought, but I do not deserve her help when I did nothing to spare her the pain of Marion's actions. Marion's mother seemed to have aged in the past few months. What a blow it must have been for Cousin Bertha to know her daughter had committed adultery, been exposed in the act, and that the management of the Mediterranean Arms had wanted to evict her on moral grounds. Maybe Roz should tell Cousin Bertha that Marion was now accepted as the new Mrs. Kramer. Most people had stopped talking about her since she and Neil were married and Sandra had moved away.

"Where does the little boy live?" Cousin Bertha asked.

Of course, Roz had to admit that Marion was pointed out to new tenants and the story told, retold, and exaggerated as once they had talked about the newly widowed neighbor—so young, so pretty, do you think she'll remarry? Well, now they knew. Roz sometimes had the impression Marion enjoyed her notoriety, considered it glamorous. She couldn't tell all that to Cousin Bertha but she answered her questions about Toby, telling the older woman that the boy lived with Sandra, who had returned to Syracuse.

The telephone rang at the other end of the apartment and Bertha Benjamin went to answer it, leaving Roz for what seemed a long time. She stared at the dark wallpaper in the kitchen, counting the number of times the pattern repeated itself above the table. While she was multiplying the number of columns, Cousin Bertha returned.

"Twice a week, my Marion calls up to ask how I am feeling."

Roz noted the mother could not restrain a note of pride that her daughter remained dutiful in this way. "Did you mention that I am here?"

"Marion does most of the talking."

So Cousin Bertha had not completely hardened her heart against Marion; if Roz could get Marion to come along the next time she visited here, perhaps there could be a complete reconciliation.

"Whatever Marion did, she is your only child."

"I know."

The resignation in Cousin Bertha's voice implied she was ready to accept her daughter on any terms. Roz wondered whether her own parents would have reacted like this and tried to figure out a way to bring mother and daughter together again.

"All is calm again in the building," Roz said.

"There was much talk about the—the divorce?"

"Most people considered it the only way. Harriet made sure to tell everyone what she saw."

"I met a Harriet," Bertha Benjamin said. "The heavy one with a little blond boy and an older girl. When my son-in-law, my first son-in-law, used to pick me up in the car and drive me to their place, my daughter and I would sit in that little park and she introduced me to all the neighbors. That Harriet is a jealous one." Cousin Bertha sighed. "I would tell my daughter, don't brag to her; she does not wish you well."

Roz could imagine Marion laughing at her mother's superstitions. "You were right."

Bertha Benjamin sighed again. She looked so old to Roz; her hands seemed frail as she lifted the sugar dish to put it away. Perhaps Cousin Bertha resented her presence because she had not stopped Harriet.

"I tried to introduce Marion to a friend of my husband, but she would not meet him. We could have kept what happened from him; we could have stopped Harriet from telling the way she saw Neil and Marion. After all, it was only one time and it was Harriet who had made sure they would be alone in Neil's apartment."

Roz knew her tea was getting cold but was too agitated to care. "I think Neil might have persuaded Sandra not to divorce him, but I guess we were foolish to think we could cover up things at that stage," Roz ended wistfully, half to herself.

"Why did I live to hear this?" Cousin Bertha moaned and tore at her hair as she grasped the meaning behind Roz's words. "A mother has to suffer, but this is too much."

"Cousin Bertha, you misunderstood me. It's not what you think." But Roz saw she could not backtrack. The tale was out and incredibly this was the first time Marion's mother had heard the truth. And I was the one, Roz thought bitterly, so concerned with having her think well of me that I hurt her worse than Marion. Marion, at least, had protected her mother from wounds too deep to heal.

"Go away, go away," Cousin Bertha screamed and Roz, frightened, hurried from the apartment.

During the long wait for her bus and the ride back to the Mediterranean Arms, Roz decided what she would do. As soon as she reached the building, she took the elevator up to the third floor instead of her own and rang Marion's doorbell.

Marion looked at her through the peephole.

"What do you want?" she asked and reluctantly opened the door chain.

"I was just at the apartment of Cousin Bertha."

"Mama didn't mention it on the telephone," Marion said as she picked up a can of glass wax and a sponge lying next to a terry cloth rag and continued rubbing it over the living room mirror, a task that Roz had evidently interrupted.

"She looked sick, Marion."

Marion continued to cover the mirror with the pink liquid, which turned to smoky white seconds after application.

"I think you should go over there right away."

"Mama doesn't want to see me."

"Please do not cover the whole mirror at once." Roz cried.

Her cousin looked at Roz, obviously wondering what caused her strange behavior, but Roz was too upset to care. "Wipe it off," she said and reached for the cloth on the floor.

"Are you crazy?"

"You must cover only one half at a time."

"What are you talking about?"

"When you clean a mirror," Roz said and began to tremble, "You must not cover the whole mirror. It is like sitting shiva if you do; it is like someone has died. Don't do it, Marion."

"I'm not superstitious," Marion said, but she began to clean off the white smoke with a tissue from her pocket while Roz worked frantically with the rag.

Roz was out of breath when she finished. "I must sit down."

"Are you all right? What's the matter with you, anyhow?"

"I am pregnant."

Marion made a tiny whistling sound through her teeth. "No wonder you're so emotional. God knows, you had me scared for a minute."

Although Roz was sitting in the white armchair now, she was dizzy and still felt sick. For a while, she forgot why she was there and leaned back, closing her eyes. Marion brought her a small glass of wine.

"I don't have any whisky, but maybe this will help."

"Thank you. You are very kind."

"Don't be silly. We are cousins, after all."

Roz drank the wine and felt a little better. If she could get the girl to visit her mother this afternoon, everything might still be made right. Surely if Roz recognized Marion was not a bad person, the mother could see it too. Old ideas died hard and to break the seventh commandment was worse in Cousin Bertha's mind than to break the fifth, but she would forgive Marion when the first shock wore off.

"Please, take a taxi and I will pay for it. It is my fault that she knows."

Marion's face lost its color as the words registered, and Roz felt sick to her stomach all over again. This was worse than she'd anticipated.

"You didn't have to tell. I'm not even pregnant and she would never have known. Mama always believed I'd become a tramp, but I proved she was wrong. I proved it once when she went berserk and took me to the doctor."

"It will be all right. Just go to see her."

"I can't go there again. Don't you understand what you did to me and to Mama? She'll never trust me again."

"Then why did you let Neil seduce you?" Roz cried, all control gone.

"I don't know," Marion said quietly.

"Tell her you are sorry."

Marion shook her head. "I can't. Maybe Aunt Lena would find some sympathy for me, but Mama would curse me."

It was fitting, Roz thought. In biblical times, the adulteress was stoned. Here they were too sophisticated to sling stones but that didn't prevent them from throwing words.

It hurt to remember how foolish she'd been about Neil. Even after an eye-opening visit to his office, Marion continued to romanticize him and ignore the cracks in his façade that gradually became visible.

Chapter 19

On Thursday, Marion had to see her dentist in Manhattan, and decided to travel from Brooklyn on the subway with Neil. They walked to the Coney Island Avenue station holding hands, and Neil bought a newspaper for each of them at the candy store under the station. Before the train jammed with riders at Kings Highway, Neil folded his paper into quarters, lengthwise, and sat calmly reading, ignoring people leaning over him and a man reading over his shoulder. Marion, who usually avoided the subway during rush hours, felt hot and perspired by the time they changed at De Kalb Avenue for the tunnel train to Wall Street. This time, they had to stand.

"Here, let me fold that for you." Neil took her Times and went through the manipulation to manage a newspaper with one hand while holding onto the strap above his head with the other hand.

"Thanks." Marion found herself very polite with Neil all the time; she was so happy to have him.

"I got a call from Syracuse at the office yesterday." Neil said.

This was no threat. Marion, in fact, often felt superior to the cast-off wife whose horizons were now limited to that upstate city. If Sandra chose to telephone Neil at the office rather than at home, so much the better.

"She's getting restless."

"And what are we supposed to do?"

Neil turned the page of his newspaper, folding each length back against its other half, and glanced at the headlines before he spoke again. "She wants to send Toby down to the city."

"I don't know anything about children."

"Kids are easy to handle. You just have to let them know who's boss."

Marion shivered despite the heat. "I hardly know Toby."

"Well, don't worry about it. If Sandra sends the kid, my mother will look after him."

It was wonderful to rely on Neil. Marion smiled gratefully at him. "Is Sandra coming back to New York, too?"

"I never know what the hell she wants."

Mr. Fontanna had re-rented the Kramers' old apartment on the fifth floor so at least she couldn't come back to the Mediterranean Arms. Marion was sure Sandra never wanted to see the place and its inhabitants again. She had, after all, agreed to the divorce terms readily enough. This last, Marion repeated aloud to Neil.

"Of course, she agreed to the settlement. That clown worked the whole thing out for her."

"Who?"

"Didn't you know her brother stuck his nose into it long enough to tell everyone what to do? Sandra always claimed I didn't like him because he has a 'strong personality,' whatever that is. But now I know why I never could stand Eddie."

Marion hadn't realized Eddie's involvement. Maybe he really did care for her, even if it seemed Neil paid an excessive amount for child support. Her husband took care of the apartment rent, bought his own clothes, and maintained the car while she paid other bills with Alec's insurance money. Although the pattern was established during the few weeks of their marriage, they hadn't discussed it.

"I wasn't going to use my vacation time traipsing off for a divorce in some oddball place and I told them if Sandra wants a divorce, she can get it herself. So she sent Eddie to talk to me and he said his sister wouldn't ask anything for herself, only for Toby, but if she had any annoyance, I'd be stuck with alimony. So I said, what the hell, in that case call a lawyer, and find out the nearest place, and I'll go."

"But how could we have gotten married if you didn't go?" Marion glanced around to see if anyone were listening to their conversation.

"Sooner or later, Sandra would've picked herself up and taken care of it."

He'd been in no hurry, Marion thought, while she'd counted the days until he left New York to establish residence for the divorce and the days until he'd returned.

"Anyhow I saved plenty of money this way," Neil said. "Not that I'm cheap, but I could use it as well as the next one."

The woman sitting directly in front of Neil, a thin, sloppily dressed blonde, stared impassively ahead with such a determined air of not listening that Marion realized she'd overheard them. She signaled to Neil and they were silent until the train pulled into Wall Street.

Everyone getting off at this stop seemed well-dressed to Marion. Most of the girls and older women wore white gloves despite the heat and it was difficult to tell the typists and file clerks from the secretaries to top executives. Along the curb, Marion saw dozens of chauffeur-driven cars standing in front of the big banks and office buildings. Sidewalks were jammed with people going to work, all walking briskly as though they had time clocks to punch, but she knew many of them were like Neil, important enough not to hurry.

"I just can't wait to see your office."

"Well, I figured you have time to kill, so you might as well meet Sidney."

Marion knew all about his partner, how he did the outside work now, but as soon as Toby was old enough, Sandra and

Neil had planned to take over the Latin American trips. She wondered if she'd accompany Neil on the next one now that Toby was no longer an obstacle.

"Will they think—I mean, did they all know Sandra?"

"Don't worry, Marion."

"But did you tell them about me?"

"Naturally. Everybody discovered why I was gone for six weeks."

This brought back the memory of what Neil implied on the subway, that he'd been in no hurry for the divorce. She now knew she owed it to Eddie that Neil married her when he did.

Marion could smell the aroma of roasting coffee through the halls of the building where Neil worked. His office was on the second floor, and he asked whether she minded walking up as the elevators were always crowded. No one before had ever been that considerate, Marion thought.

The large room they walked into was dominated by a round table; three men sitting there looked up at their entrance. Marion was startled to see one of them, a short nearly bald man, spit before he rose to meet them.

"Tasting coffee," Neil explained

"It's lousy," the short man said.

"Marion, this is Sidney Meltzer. Sid, my wife Marion."

Neil's partner extended his hand. "You should've been here fifteen minutes ago. I had to roast it myself."

"I'm sorry. Marion came in to see her dentist."

"On the Street?"

"No, uptown."

"Why don't you go and check through the mail. Betty's tied up with a contract."

Neil walked over to a desk, set flush with the back wall of the room and started to leaf through letters waiting there for him. After a while, he seemed to forget Marion was at the office today and sat down, rapidly slitting envelopes, opening letters and cable copies, and stacking them into two piles— one of which he soon carried into the other room. For the first time, Marion noticed that Sidney Meltzer had a separate, private office. She asked Neil about it in a whisper when he emerged.

"Oh, that's just for the foreigners."

"What do you mean?"

"There has to be a headman for the Latin Americans, so they feel they're dealing with the main firm representative." Neil leafed through two heavy books at the far edge of his desk, which he soon brought forward and after sharpening a pencil wrote on a clipboard, referring constantly to the stack of cables and the books.

"But I thought you were an equal partner."

"I just told you, it's only a convenience for our customers."

"I don't think it's fair."

"You women are all alike. What has 'fair' to do with business? If the firm makes more money with me sitting out here, then this is where I sit."

The secretary approached Neil's desk and handed him some papers. "Say Neil, Mr. Meltzer wants you to drop everything and take this contract over to Martinson's."

"Let's go," Neil said to Marion. "I can walk you back to the subway after I deliver this."

They walked out of the office and down the steps while Neil muttered about never seeming to catch up before something new erupted.

"Well, why do you have to deliver the contract?"

"We still take a lot of stuff around by hand on the Street when we can't afford to waste time. Now this contract must be signed by the buyer immediately so we can send copies out to our shipper without losing an extra day."

Marion listened, remembering that the secretary had called him by his first name while speaking respectfully of his partner as 'Mr. Meltzer.'

"Doesn't the firm have anyone else to use as a messenger boy?"

"He was probably out someplace."

"You shouldn't have to substitute for him."

"What the hell! I don't mind." He leaned towards her and kissed her cheek, a gesture she'd considered so romantic during the years she'd observed him with Sandra. Now when she was the recipient, it appeared like an offering.

Fotolia #69030946 - Brooklyn old buildings and Manhattan Bridge in Dumbo © blvdone

Unbearable guilt. That's how Marion remembered that time. Even now, forty years later, she felt her eyes tear at the memory.

Chapter 20

By the time Marion finished with the dentist and spent the afternoon in the stores, drifting from Ohrbach's to Gimbel's to Sak's 34th, she'd forgotten her surprise at the reality of Neil's job and her disappointment in him. She was tired and took one of the special taxis, crowded with other shoppers, back to Brooklyn. At her building, the doorman helped with her packages and she tipped him a quarter.

In a hurry to put away her purchases and prepare dinner, Marion was grateful to find both lobby and elevator deserted. On the third floor, an overhead light had burned out, giving the hallway a gloomy air and making it difficult to see the keyhole. I should call down to Perry, she thought but was too rushed to bother.

The telephone rang while Marion was hanging up the new suit she'd bought for the Jewish High Holy Days, so she ignored it. Since the message about Alec had come one afternoon as she prepared dinner, she'd never again been eager to grab the telephone receiver.

Neil arrived shortly after six, in a very good mood, admired the olive suit, the blouse which blended perfectly with it, and a white hat he insisted looked like a beehive.

"What no shoes, no handbag?"

"A handbag you don't take to shul."

"You're planning to go to shul for the holidays? Even Sandra didn't bother with that."

"If you don't want to go, I don't care very much, but I need new clothes for the holidays anyhow."

"It's your money," Neil said. "Suit yourself."

This time when the phone rang, Neil answered it. "I'll get Marion, hold on," she heard him say. She figured it was one of her friends and prepared to say they were starting dinner and she would call back.

"Oh, Aunt Lena. What's the matter?"

There were no words from Aunt Lena but Marion could hear her sobbing. She must have had an argument with Mama, Marion thought. Maybe about me. "It will be all right," she said. "Don't get upset."

"Come over. Quick, quick." Aunt Lena told her and hung up.

"Are you going?" Neil asked while they ate the lamb chops she had broiled for dinner.

"They're always fighting and then one or the other of them calls up in hysterics."

"You know them better than I do."

"I'll telephone after we finish eating and see if they've calmed down."

But again, Aunt Lena refused to say what had happened, telling Marion only that she was needed.

At the door to her mother's apartment, Marion rang the bell and waited. A stranger came to let her in; no, she'd seen this woman before at some family affair—a wedding or a funeral or something. Her name was Sarah, she remembered. All at once, Marion started to shiver. She wanted to shout for her mother but called for Aunt Lena instead.

"Your aunt is lying down. Did she tell you yet?"

And Marion knew it was true. She suddenly found herself running through the apartment to see whether all the rooms were empty. She found Aunt Lena crying in her room.

"How did it happen?" Marion asked. Her mouth was dry and she had to swallow twice to bring the words out.

"Another stroke." The strange woman had followed Marion and answered before her aunt could. "Your mother didn't suffer, Marion. It was very quick."

"Where is she?"

"We tried to reach you all day," Aunt Lena sobbed.

"It wouldn't have done any good," the other woman said. "Your aunt sent for an ambulance and they took your mother to the hospital, but it was too late."

"I should have been here."

"Look dear, there wasn't anything that could be done."

"My sister never hurt anybody," Aunt Lena sobbed. "She had such a hard life and then they go and aggravate her to death."

Marion, who'd felt numbed from the moment she entered the apartment, froze as the import of her aunt's words reached her.

It can't be anything I've done, Marion insisted to herself but remembered Roz's report of her last visit with Mama.

"All that aggravation; all that aggravation."

"Aunt Lena, please. People don't die from that. Don't say it was because of me."

Her aunt seemed to pull herself together. "I did not mean that, child. It was the shock."

"What do we do now? I don't know what to do."

"The Rabbi has been here; the funeral is tomorrow. Sarah is helping us to make all the arrangements. We will begin to sit shiva after the funeral and you, Marion, will live here for the week of mourning."

Marion vaguely remembered visiting people, in her mother's company, who'd lost family members. They spent a week at home, wearing slippers and sitting on low wooden benches. As Roz had reminded her, people in mourning covered the mirrors. She hadn't done any of the prescribed rituals for Alec because she'd visited Mama in the hospital every day. Aunt Lena had handled everything that time, while today Aunt Lena was obviously too agitated to think about the details. It was hard to see her affected this way when she used to fight with Mama all the time. Like me, Marion thought, she really loved Mama despite the arguments. She noticed Aunt Lena's careful observation of her.

"Did you ever realize what your mother felt? Did you ever understand?"

"She always treated everyone else better than me. When Roz came here, Mama waited on her."

"She wanted you to feel this was still your home. She used to tell me, 'Don't act like Marion is company.'"

"I didn't know that," Marion said.

"And you didn't know Bertha was torn apart by guilt. It was like driving a car and killing a pedestrian or any other kind of accidental killing—unbearable, unbelievable guilt. That's how your Mama spent the last months of her life."

"I thought she didn't care," Marion cried out in anguish.

"You never thought about her at all."

Marion walked slowly into the kitchen, remembering all the times Mama had been at work there. "Marion, you make the tea," Mama would say or "Marion you do the dishes." She would gladly do it now.

It was important to call Neil, Marion thought numbly and couldn't remember for a moment why. She dialed her telephone number and Neil answered on the first ring. "What was the fuss over there?"

"Mama had another stroke. She died this afternoon." Marion tried to keep her voice steady.

"That's tough, kid."

The words sounded hollow, though Marion knew he meant to console her. "I'll have to stay. Can you pack up a few things for me? There's an overnight case on top of the linen closet."

"Stay a while and I'll pick you up around eleven o'clock. There's no reason for you to be there overnight."

"Neil, the funeral is tomorrow, early, so it's all over before Shabbos. Then I have to sit shiva all week except Shabbos."

"Are you serious?"

"I must give Mama that respect. Please hurry over. I can't talk about it now."

"I'll be there in twenty minutes, but you can't expect me to stay alone for a week. Better have it all settled before I get there."

He hung up. Marion stared at the telephone, wondering if Neil really would try to stop her from following the orthodox ritual. What would Aunt Lena say? For that matter, would there be a commotion when Neil came to the apartment?

Aunt Lena was quiet when Marion said she would go home with Neil to pack some things for the week.

Her aunt seemed resigned to whatever life would bring now that her sister was gone, calmly watching while Sarah wrote down the name of the funeral home where Marion was to be the next morning.

"Go early and you can see your Mama in the casket before everyone arrives," Sarah said, rubbing her chin nervously.

"Yes, yes. I will." Marion found herself making the same gesture.

"Why do you run off so early?"

"Sarah, leave her alone. She just got married. The husband wants her to come home."

Marion stared at her aunt. She had sounded like Mama, her tone exactly the one Mama used when referring to Neil.

"Well, he'll have to do without her during the shiva."

"Would you like some tea, Marion?" Aunt Lena asked.

"Sit, sit. I'll do it," Sarah said. She rushed out of the bedroom and they could hear her opening closets in the kitchen.

"That woman will know what's in every drawer before the night is over," Aunt Lena said. "She's staying with me so there is no reason for you to remain, but Marion, this I tell you. You will give your mother the proper respect, no matter what that new husband of yours says."

Marion didn't have to argue with Aunt Lena about it because Neil arrived just then and she left with him, but she found herself in the same discussion with Neil on the way home. He was sorry about her mother, but he was not going to remain by himself all week.

"You know it has to be done." Marion couldn't tell him Aunt Lena was the only one in the world who cherished her right or wrong. She refused to lose that person's regard.

'I don't know any such thing."

"Look Neil, I feel awful. Take me away somewhere for a rest right after the funeral and we can avoid all of this."

"You expect me to take time off now?"

"I need you." Marion held back her tears. Couldn't he see how important it was for them to get away? She was willing to forego Latin American trips. Anything. She would go anywhere to be away from here.

"I took off six weeks to get the damn divorce. Now Sidney is entitled to equal vacation time."

"Well, then let him take it."

"He doesn't want it."

"Can't we make it a business trip? To Brazil or somewhere. You always said you would be making the foreign tours if not for Toby."

Neil seemed embarrassed. "I'm sorry. We agreed. He's the outside man and I'm the inside man."

Did Sandra know, Marion nearly asked aloud, but she swallowed the words. I guess I'm finally growing up, she thought. I won't see myself as a perpetual eighteen- or nineteen-year old anymore the way Eddie claimed.

"Stop looking through me the way Sandra did. What do you want? What in God's name do you girls expect from me?"

"Never mind, Neil." His eyebrows, which always gelled together when Neil laughed, joined the same way when he scowled, Marion noticed, but he still looked incredibly handsome.

"We might be able to swing a weekend in the Catskills later on," he said as they reached their apartment.

"If we stay in Brooklyn now, I have to be with my aunt. She's getting older. The strain could kill her, too." Marion started to weep uncontrollably, wishing all the time that Neil would leave the room. No, what she really wanted was comfort, but he seemed so awkward, standing by without a word. Finally, he put his hand on her shoulder.

"I never dreamed it would be this way," Marion said.

"This will pass, just as Alec's death did."

Neil's tactless consolation upset her more. He seemed to have a genius for saying the wrong words. Didn't he know what he represented—that she'd forgotten Alec quickly enough to live with someone else in the same apartment and the same bed? I replaced my husband, she wanted to say, but there's no way .to replace a mother.

"All right. If you can't take me away, I understand," Marion said again. "But I must sit shiva."

"That's impossible."

She couldn't understand his refusal in the light of all the years she'd known him and Sandra. With Sandra, Neil seemed to do whatever she asked of him. At least, that was what Sandra had led her to believe. But here he was turning Marion down again. She'd have to make the best of it.

"Eat at your family's just this week?"

"You know my mother has bursitis." Neil said. "This is for your sake, to keep you occupied and away from all the old women sitting around that apartment telling you how many years they've known your mother."

Maybe I want to hear them say good things about Mama, Marion thought, but she didn't argue with Neil. He couldn't understand that the blow of Mama's death was intensified because she knew Aunt Lena counted her responsible. Aunt Lena had always hated it when Marion blamed Mama for Alec's death. Now Marion, caught up by similar circumstances, realized what it had been like for her mother.

Fotolia #32107417 - Grand Army Plaza in Prospect Park, Brooklyn © SeanPavonePhoto

Roz was the one who first made Marion come to grips with her shallow outlook and selfishness. Now, she couldn't believe she had been that empty-headed young woman who never looked beyond the superficial.

Chapter 21

R oz Geller's first reaction to the death of Cousin Bertha was fear that she'd lose her baby because of the shock. But she became ashamed when she saw how awful Marion looked. If I feel responsible, and I do, Roz thought, how much worse it must be for Marion.

Her clothes, which she'd managed to squeeze into only the day before were too tight and she put on her new orchid maternity dress. At Cousin Bertha's apartment, Roz walked in without greeting anyone, the way you were supposed to act when people were mourning. Marion perched on a wooden stool and although Roz noticed right away that her eyes were not reddened, they looked puffy from lack of sleep. This was the first time Roz had seen her cousin without makeup and with her hair just brushed back out of her face instead of elaborately styled, but with her exotic eyes and high cheekbones, nothing could disguise her beauty.

"Where is your aunt? I hope she is not ill."

"Aunt Lena is lying down. I never knew she cared so much for Mama; she can't seem to do anything without her."

"They were, after all, sisters."

"Yes, but all the years, they..."

Roz knew Marion would not talk frankly for she was no longer trusted. "When you fight with somebody, it does not always mean there is no love. I have had already an argument with Marty, and we are married only a few months." This was information Roz would rather not have revealed to anyone, but she offered it to help Marion.

"Don't you see? Mama and I never got along, either."

"Exactly what I am trying to say, Marion. You must know that it does not mean anything, that you loved her just as your aunt did."

"While I was growing up, I never understood why Aunt Lena lived here with us when Mama was so gruff with her. I used to ask her, 'Why don't you just move out? I will, as soon as I'm old enough.' Now, I've discovered Mama supported Aunt Lena all these years even though she barely had enough income for herself."

Roz looked around at the covered mirror over the old-fashioned mantel and shuddered. "That is no surprise to me. Cousin Bertha was good to my family also."

"You were right about the mirror."

"It is just a superstition."

"But I should have paid attention to you."

"What will you do now?" Roz asked to change the subject.

"What can I do?" Marion stood up and walked around the living room in her slippered feet and Roz watched, waiting for the right time to present her idea to her cousin.

"You plan to remain in the same apartment?"

"Of course. I love the Arms and now that Sandra's upstate, nothing in the building will upset me."

"But those other women, does their talk not bother you?"

"Them!" Marion shook her head. "They'll soon find other gossip."

"What about this apartment?"

"Are you hinting that Neil and I should move in here with Aunt Lena? I never heard anything so foolish."

"But your aunt cannot keep up this place alone."

"What can I do?" Marion cried out.

Roz knew she must try to help, not foolishly as when she'd tried to introduce Marion to one of Marty's friends, but with courage and finality. "Do you want to feel as bad about your aunt one day as you do about Cousin Bertha?"

There was no answer from Marion, who stood in front of the draped mirror staring at it as though she could see through the white sheet that covered it.

"You can tell me that I have no right to give you advice, that I am also to blame for what happened, but that is why I must speak up."

"Do you think I'm so rich that I can support Aunt Lena?"

"It is not my business, but all the women in our building say you live on the income from the insurance of your first husband."

"That shows how much they know."

"It is only gossip?"

"I'll tell this to you, Roz, and now even Neil knows it. I've lived on the principal, not the income."

It took Roz a few minutes to realize what her cousin was saying. "It is all spent now?"

"Not all."

"But you are married again. And to an executive."

"Yes. A big shot with big child support payments," Marion said bitterly.

"Whatever you have, it is more than your aunt has."

"For all I know, Mama provided for her. It would have been like Mama to do that. I'm learning all about that side to her now."

"No, Marion, my sister left her money to you." Aunt Lena had come into the room without Marion, who remained in front of the shrouded mirror, or Roz noticing her.

"It should have been for you," Marion burst out, "Then there would be no decision for me to make."

"When you were married to Alec, Bertha made a will leaving her small annuity to me because she knew he would take care of you. You will find that the latest will was made out only a short time ago. She was afraid to trust your new husband."

"God knows, I didn't ask for it."

"But the income, though it is small, will be a help to you."

"And you?"

Roz waited with Marion to see what Aunt Lena's plans were. She had spoken up, but her new-found courage quickly deserted her when the older woman came into the room.

"I shall get a job."

"What?"

Roz could sense Marion's struggle to refrain from hurting her aunt with a wrong word. But what a magnificent person, Roz thought, to consider going out to work at her age in order to protect Marion.

"Aunt Lena, it isn't easy to find work today unless you're trained. You need some special skill."

"One could take a typing course."

"I wouldn't want to think of you struggling to compete with the new high school graduates."

"About fifteen years ago, I found a job with a brokerage. They called me a filing clerk. But your mother wanted me to move in with her. She said she was lonely."

Roz implored Marion with her eyes. She wanted to shout, "Give it to her. It is only money and she cared about you all your life." She saw Marion glance her way and nod, as though she understood without words.

"If the annuity comes to me, I'm going to sign it right over to you."

"I cannot let you do that, child."

"But you know I have plenty of money from Alec's insurance. I have nothing to worry about with an income like that." Marion put her arms around her aunt and patted her shoulder. "Go and lie down again. I'll take care of everything."

Roz thought about Marion all the way home on the bus. The girl had made a complete mess of things, but she was not really a bad person; she seemed ready to make amends wherever possible.

Fearing she might be caught up by the same atmosphere that had overwhelmed Marion, Roz intended to walk past the gold and white Mediterranean Arms playground without stopping, but Harriet called to her.

Harriet and Bobbie were knitting furiously as though they were in a race with each other. Roz saw their eyes widen as they realized simultaneously she was in maternity clothes.

"You didn't tell me you were pregnant," Harriet said.

"It is now noticeable without any speeches from me." Roz smiled at her stocky neighbor because she could see Harriet was hurt.

"When are you due?"

"Early next year."

"And you never said a word. What are you ashamed about?"

"Now Harriet, leave her alone." Roberta's baby started crying and she took him out of the carriage. "Babies are cute, everyone knows that, but you should have waited. This one has ruined my life. If not for him, I could have modeled or maybe even broken into television."

"Don't blame the baby for that, Bobbie. You never got anywhere before he was born."

"That shows how much you know," Roberta retorted childishly. "Jerome has contacts, but it was just my luck to become pregnant the minute we began our honeymoon."

"Let's see," Harriet shrieked. "You're married a year and the baby is four months old."

"He was premature. You can see how tiny he is for his age."

"I guess Roz will have a premature baby, too," Harriet said. "They seem to run in the building. Now, in my case Phyllis is six years old and Shelley and I have been married nearly ten years, so you girls can't find anything to gossip about."

"Who's gossiping?" Roberta asked. "You're the biggest yenta in the building anyhow."

"Hit you where it hurt, didn't I?"

Roz, listening to them, wondered how the poised ladies she had envied could have degenerated into shrill name-callers. And these two were considered best friends. With her, she knew, they would show less mercy.

She was right. Harriet suddenly lost interest in baiting Roberta and turned back to her. "What month did you say you're in?"

Even Aunt Lena hadn't been so blunt although her curiosity was probably greater. She could not bring herself to tell Harriet that it was none of her business. "Let us wait and see," Roz finally said.

"Looks like you and your cousin both had to get married."

Roz gasped. "You are mistaken."

"I saw it with my own eyes, didn't I?"

"If you mean what happened with Marion and Neil, we have no right to condemn her. She has suffered enough."

"Is she taking her mother's death hard?" Harriet leaned forward with her mouth avidly moving. "Did you see her? Was she crying?"

"Don't be so morbid," Roberta said.

"Look Bobbie, if I want your opinion, I'll ask for it."

"My cousin has dignity that will carry her through, and I would appreciate it if you do not talk against her again in my presence. We have all caused her enough trouble."

"So, she winds up with a handsome husband, plenty of money, and everything she wanted. You don't have to worry about Marion."

Roz sat silently watching the few children in the sandbox. She had wanted so desperately to belong, to be just like her neighbors. To Roz, they had appeared as examples of the Americanization she strained for, of the way Marty would want her to be. Now she looked at Harriet and at the slender, girlish Roberta and thought that five years from now and ten years from now they would be sitting here as they were now, still commenting on every passerby.

Is this the way I want my life to be, Roz wondered and got up and walked out of the playground. As she left, she could hear Harriet asking Roberta how many veal chops she had to cook for Jerome.

In the distance, the path along Sheepshead Bay stretched for blocks, tree-shaded and lined with gray benches, but the city's gray ones looked better to Roz now than the gold and white ones she'd admired at the Mediterranean Arms. She crossed the street to Sheepshead Bay.

How painful it had been to see Sandra again and to realize how much Toby missed his father.

Chapter 22

Sandra came to the apartment a few days after Bertha Benjamin's funeral. In her nubby pink suit, appearing unsophisticated and little girlish, she made Marion feel very worldly by comparison. Toby was with his mother.

Nervously, Marion offered Sandra a seat and crossed to the other side of the room where she peered out the window while waiting to hear what Sandra would say. Toby climbed onto the back of a white velvet chair and sat there swinging his legs while Marion watched helplessly, unwilling to admonish him. His mother finally told him to get down.

"Why don't you park Toby at your dinette table with a pencil and some paper?" Sandra suggested.

Marion quickly handed writing materials over. "This is for you, Toby."

"Chief Thundercloud."

"Neil brought him a headdress and tomahawk when he visited Toby last week. Now this Indian business is worse than ever."

Careful not to mention this was her first knowledge of the visit, Marion fumbled with a venetian blind for a moment, shading the room. Of course, he visits his son, she told herself. That proves he really is kind and considerate. She wondered what Sandra wanted, but the blonde girl sat primly and silently on the sofa in contrast to the way she used to perch there.

"Will you have some coffee?" Marion asked, surprised she could speak normally despite the hysterical laughter that wanted to well inside her throat.

"Don't bother."

"Are you waiting to see Neil? He won't be home for another hour."

"Yes. I know what time he leaves the office." Sandra said drily.

Marion searched for conversation. "It's getting pretty windy outside now. Neil says we're going to have an early winter."

"Are we reduced to talking about the weather?" Sandra asked. She stared at Marion. "Don't the women in the playground bother you? They're like a Greek chorus commenting on everything we do. I thought you'd take another apartment, but I guess this building has always meant too much to you."

"I did want to move. There was an empty on the first floor, but my lease wasn't up."

"And besides you'll have to pay rent on 5G until Mr. Fontanna finds someone else for it."

Marion shrugged. "Only for this month and next month plus a paint job for the new people."

"That must have irked Neil."

"Neil has been grand," Marion stated flatly.

"You don't have to cover up for him the way I did. 'Neil says this and Neil says that.' I know all about him."

"I said Neil's been grand," Marion repeated.

"The circles under your eyes are darker than ever. Do you really claim to be happy?"

"Did you come here to torment me? How did you find out that Mama is dead?"

Sandra reeled back against the sofa. "I didn't know it. I swear."

"You don't have to lie to me."

"Our present relationship is such, Marion, that there's no need for me to lie anymore. We're not emotionally involved in friendship."

"I'm sorry, Sandra."

"You're always sorry afterwards."

"I should have placed a higher value on our friendship; you fooled me about many things, didn't you?"

With a shrewd glance, Sandra seemed to understand what Marion's apology cost her. "It's pointless going into that now."

Again, Marion wanted to ask why Sandra had come but they were interrupted by Toby, his face and fingers smeared with ink.

"I need something to play with. The paper is all used up."

"Good lord, Marion! Did you give him a pen?"

Marion, who'd picked up the first thing handy, a pen and memo pad that hung next to her kitchen telephone, started to apologize but changed her mind. She can't expect me to know about children, she told herself.

"All right, Chief Thundercloud, back into the kitchen with you," Sandra told her little boy. "Do you have any dry cereal he can munch on? That will keep him occupied."

It was now past five o'clock, Marion noticed when she returned to the kitchen. Neil would be home within the hour, and she had to start his dinner soon. If only she could get rid of Sandra before he walked into the apartment, all would be well.

"My brother insists I have a responsibility toward you," Sandra said when Marion took up her post by the window again.

"I would have expected him to say the opposite."

"That's not Eddie's way. He feels that I injured you."

Marion moved to the side of the coffee table opposite Sandra. "Why did you let that miserable Harriet use you? You and your brother are perceptive people, aware of things I'd never notice. Surely you suspected."

"It was the easiest way."

"But why? Why wreck your life for a whim?"

"Look at me, Marion. Have I been destroyed?"

"You seem the same as you always have." Marion sighed. "That's not exactly it; the pink suit fooled me. You've grown more sure of yourself, more confident. I would have expected the opposite."

"Many times, you've told me that you couldn't bear to believe your life was going to remain the same forever and every time I heard you, it echoed in my own mind. I despised myself for it, Marion, but there it was."

Marion wanted to deny Sandra's words, but the little boy ran into the living room again before she could speak. He had a fist full of snapshots.

"It's my daddy. Look!" Toby deposited the photographs in Sandra's lap. "Where is my daddy? I want him."

Her knees suddenly crumbled and Marion was forced to sink to the carpet and lean her head against the coffee table. Not this, she thought. I can't bear it.

"You'll see daddy next Sunday," Sandra was saying. "Now go back and play, and stay away from the cabinets and drawers in there this time."

When Toby had gone, Sandra walked around the coffee table to Marion and pulled her to her feet. "This isn't why I came here today. I never wanted a scene."

"Why did you come?" Marion's voice emerged as a whisper.

"It was Eddie's idea. He said that one of us had to do it and it would be better if I were the one; I agreed."

She gazed at her, Marion realized now, the same way Sandra had all those times she tried to comfort her after Alec's death. Marion never understood until now the compassion that look held.

"Now listen to me all the way through without interruption," Sandra said. "You've borne a terrible burden of guilt for nearly a year now, blaming yourself for the unavoidable reaction against your mother brought on by Alec's death. And you haven't been willing to face it. You've been afraid that you're some sort of hard-hearted monster because you couldn't help blaming your mother. I know you sometimes tormented yourself because you wished it had been the other way around, that Alec had lived even if your mother were the victim instead." Holding up a warning hand, Sandra stopped Marion from breaking into her analysis and continued.

"When I came here, I didn't know it was all over. I wanted to tell you there was no need for you to have me on your conscience, too.

"We've talked it over many times, my brother and I, and we finally agreed one of us had to take that burden from you."

Were they really trying to help her, Marion wondered. She tried to picture herself acting as decently under the circumstances and failed.

"I didn't expect my marriage to end so publicly," Sandra said wryly, "but aside from the time and place, everything went exactly as I hoped it would."

"But why?"

"There's no point in my going into reasons. I want you to be happy with Neil, not to be prejudiced by me."

"It killed Mama when she found out about that afternoon in your apartment." Marion saw the shock in Sandra's eyes. "I can't express what I feel about your trying to ease my guilt but you've come too late."

"I wish I could help you."

Marion shook her head. When she could speak without the danger of crying in front of Sandra, she met the other girl's glance. "What will you do now?"

"For a while, I didn't have any plans other than living back home again. But Syracuse wasn't the way I remembered it or maybe my outlook has changed. Anyhow, Eddie's going to Spain on an exchange fellowship and I'm planning to tag along."

"Spain! But you never particularly wanted to travel."

"I've been classified as the little small town hick in your eyes for years, but it's different now. I'm in that romantically interesting category you were part of—young widows and divorcées have appeal for men. I intend to have a good time and I don't expect to return to Brooklyn."

"Does Neil know?"

"He's no part of my life anymore."

"Then if this is really the last time we'll meet, I want to ask you one more favor. Will you leave before Neil comes home and finds you here?"

"Are you afraid?"

Unable to explain the uneasiness she felt at the thought of witnessing a meeting between Sandra, Neil and Toby, Marion asked herself why she'd spoken, knowing the other girl would misinterpret her motives.

"We no longer have an effect on each other, Marion. I assure you there's nothing."

And that, Marion admitted to herself, was exactly what she feared seeing. Sandra and Neil had been married for six years. She was unable to imagine how everything between them could have evaporated.

Marion restarted the ignition and pulled away from the Mediterranean Arms. Reliving her choices of forty years before not only caused burning regret, but also the realization she'd been no more capable of understanding the genuine in life than in the Arms itself.

Chapter 23

The week had fallen into a pattern; Marion left early each morning for Aunt Lena's apartment, remained there all day following the forms of the shiva, but returned home in late afternoon to have dinner ready for Neil. Some of the older people who made condolence calls were shocked by this arrangement, but Marion noticed Aunt Lena made no attempt to defend her.

At the time of Alec's death, Marion had wandered numbly from the funeral to the hospital where her mother lay partially paralyzed from her stroke. The daze lasted for weeks. Now, the first numbness wore off quickly to be replaced by deep sorrow.

When Marion returned to her apartment toward the end of that week, she felt near the breaking point. She was so tired that on first unlocking the apartment door, the disorder didn't register. She'd collapsed onto one of the white velvet occasional chairs with her head in her hands and remained that way for a time before realizing the apartment had been ransacked. All the months Marion had worried about a break-in, she'd been near hysteria just at the possibility of one. Now that it actually happened, she was too weary even to see what was missing or to call for help.

Neil arrived about half an hour later. "Have the police been here?"

"I haven't called yet."

"Well, what are you waiting for?" He went to the telephone and pointedly took care of it himself.

"It won't do any good," Marion said. "No one in the building has gotten back a thing that was stolen."

"What's missing?"

"I didn't get to check it out."

He grumbled under his breath about having to do everything himself and went into the bedroom, where she could hear him opening and closing drawers and closets. "Is your beaver coat in storage?"

"No, I didn't bother this year."

"Then, it's gone. Also, your jewel box has been emptied out."

"Some of it was costume jewelry."

"But what about the real stuff. You had plenty of the real stuff from Alec."

Maybe I didn't deserve to keep those jewels, Marion thought and was glad she had her first wedding band and engagement ring in her handbag.

"Look at that," Neil said. "They took that antique cigarette case you kept here on the coffee table, but didn't touch the spice box Eddie gave you. Shows you it's a piece of junk." Neil tossed it from one hand to the other.

"Give it to me."

"You mean my little brother-in-law made an impression on you after all. Wait until you see the letter I got from Sandra today."

"What does she say?"

"Sandra is planning to go to Spain with Eddie."

Marion suppressed her admission she'd already been told this by Sandra. She imagined Eddie approaching the castles, the caves, the culture and atmosphere of Spain with his earnest appreciation. And Sandra would now see something of the world, even if with her brother rather than Neil. Sandra would probably spend only a short time there—she was after all only Eddie's sister. But I could have stayed, Marion thought.

The doorbell rang. "There's Mr. Fontanna," Neil said and brought Marion back to reality.

"Are you sure someone broke in?" Mr. Fontanna asked. His face was red and he kept rubbing a finger behind his right ear.

"Of course we're sure. Can't you see what this place looks like? Even the seat cushions were lifted, as if they wanted the nickels and pennies that fall out of our pockets into the upholstery," Neil said.

"Why don't the police do something?" Marion asked.

Mr. Fontanna rubbed his ear again. "Yours is the second today. The cops have been here all afternoon questioning people. Whoever it is gets nervier all the time."

"So they make a big fat report and the burglaries continue," Neil said.

"What do you want from me? I do the best I can, but I'm the one whose head is going to roll after today's business."

"It has to be an inside job," Neil said.

"That's what the cops think."

The doorbell rang again, insistently blasting until it was answered. This is unbearable, Marion thought. I should've had chimes installed.

Two uniformed policemen stood in the doorway, holding onto Joey Fontanna. "This yours, lady?"

Marion examined the gold choker that was held out to her. "Yes."

"Joey, what's the matter?"

"What do you think, Pop?"

"Your boy's been pushing his luck," one of the officers said. "Three in one day. We caught him coming into your apartment with two transistor radios and a typewriter."

"Ah, you never would have caught me if I didn't start rushing the jobs to get to Las Vegas. I thought you guys left the building an hour ago."

"It must be a mistake."

"If that's want you want to think, Pop, go ahead, but you can see they got me."

"I guess I thought it was Perry, the janitor, all the time but I never did anything about it," Mr. Fontanna said.

"Well, it was me, Pop."

"What kind of life is this?" Mr. Fontanna asked, gazing imploringly at Marion and Neil. "The children are killing the parents."

Marion saw the grief on Mr. Fontanna's face and almost wished his son hadn't been caught. She'd rather have lost the things he'd stolen forever than realize this must have been how Mama looked when Roz blurted out the story of her own actions.

"You don't have to take it personally," Joey Fontanna said and left the apartment with one officer and his father while the other stayed behind to complete a report on the break-in.

Marion watched Neil as he answered questions and saw that he was untouched by the Fontannas' tragedy. Instead, he seemed curiously elated through his personal involvement in the apprehension of a criminal. How strange, she thought. She'd always gotten the impression from Sandra that Neil was a particularly sensitive person. Her own description of him would have contained the word "kind," but tonight he'd witnessed the tragedy of a family without being moved.

"Glad that's over," Neil said when the policeman left. "I'm starved."

Marion quickly put two steaks into the broiler and started water boiling for rice. This is my fault, she thought. I've talked with him only on a superficial level, the way that disturbed Eddie so much.

"How was everything at your aunt's today?" Neil asked. He had followed her into the kitchen, and leaned against the refrigerator watching her prepare dinner.

Marion was reminded of the time Neil had come downstairs near midnight at her call and how thrilling the sight of him in this same pose had been then. They'd talked seriously that night.

"Neil, did you see his face."

"Joey's? What a two-bit punk he turned out to be!"

"Mr. Fontanna's face."

"We'll read about him in the papers tomorrow, saying 'my Joey was always a good boy.'"

"But Neil, he'll never get over this; Joey is his only child, just as I was Mama's only child." Marion started to cry, leaning her head against the refrigerator, a few inches away from Neil.

"Look, kid. You've got nothing to cry about. I told you before that Sandra and I weren't getting along."

"This will haunt me for a long time."

"You'll get over it soon."

But the weeks went by and Marion's despair remained. Mr. Fontanna moved out, and a firm of realtors began acting as rental agents for the Mediterranean Arms. The women in the playground were busy discussing fall styles and buying clothes for the Jewish New Year, but Marion had no desire to shop for more new things or even to add to the outfit she'd bought the day Mama died. She felt herself sinking into the apathetic state she'd reached before Neil showed his interest in her and was afraid this time there'd be no way to escape. What a waste that would be! She'd told Mama she couldn't live without Neil and now, with Mama dead because of her actions, she was more unhappy than before.

The problem was what to do now. If giving up Neil would help, she'd willingly do it, but that wouldn't make any difference. In fact, since she'd sacrificed so much to have him, it would be the worst admission of defeat.

She must try harder to make the marriage a success and not let Neil sense her disappointment in him, the way she'd felt when she'd asked him to say Kaddish prayers for her mother. Neil had refused. In the end, Aunt Lena helped her find an old man at the synagogue who'd say the mourners' prayers for a small payment.

But when Neil came home that evening, despite her resolution, Marion found herself asking him to accompany her to Rosh Hashonah services.

"Are you serious? I haven't been inside a synagogue since my Bar Mitzvah."

"It's important to me this year."

"Are you suddenly getting religion?"

"No, but Mama believed in all this, and it's the least I can do out of respect for her memory."

"You want religion, it's okay with me, but don't expect an escort."

"It would help to know you were there with me."

"Come on, kid. I have enough problems of my own."

"What's the matter, Neil? Is it your job?"

"No, I don't have to worry about the partnership. Sid can't do without me."

Marion waited for him to go on, determined to sympathize and help him. She would do anything to feel as close to Neil as on the night he'd comforted her after her nightmare.

"Sandra's shifting Toby to me."

"What? I mean, didn't she get full custody?"

"Naturally. But she's going to Europe and she doesn't want the responsibility."

"She's giving up Toby?"

"Sandra never cared much for either one of us. So she got rid of me and now it's Toby's turn."

Marion watched Neil fill his pipe. She'd loved to see this when he was married to Sandra; it had seemed so virile. "Your mother will surely take him."

"Sandra called her first. But Mom has bursitis and she's getting too old to look after a little boy. She said as long as I married again, I should take him."

A nerve in Marion's cheek started twitching and she put her hand up to hide it from Neil. "I don't know anything about children."

"He's an easy kid to handle. You can just take him down to the playground and keep an eye on him, but he'll amuse himself."

Marion saw herself sitting in the playground day after day with the bitter-faced women. "When they shift Toby to you, it's really me they mean."

"What's the difference? He's mine and if Sandra won't keep him, I have no choice."

"Oh, Neil." Marion sat down beside him on the sofa and rested her head on his shoulder.

"Look out, Marion! Can't you see I'm filling a pipe."

"Yes, yes. I see."

"Anyhow, we don't have to take Toby forever."

"Yes," Marion repeated.

"It's only for one goddamned year."

Only a year, Marion thought. And her obligation to Toby would end but she would have Neil for the rest of her life. It seemed a long time since that had been her most fervent desire.

RENÉE B. HOROWITZ, a retired Arizona State University (ASU) professor, is a Brooklyn native who now lives in Scottsdale, Arizona.

Bitter Moon Over Brooklyn is a departure from Renée's Rx series of mystery novels and her stand-alone mystery, *The Write Way to Murder*.

We all know that Brooklyn is unique. In *Bitter Moon Over Brooklyn*, Renée brings to life an amalgam of the many characters who were part of her Brooklyn apartment-dwelling life.

Her Rx series presents an authentic, behind-the-scenes look at pharmacy, inspired not only by her pharmacist husband, but also by both their pharmacist dads. Look for *Rx for Murder, Deadly Rx, and Rx Alibi,* the Ruthie Kantor Morris mysteries. She is also a founding member and past president of the Desert Sleuths Chapter of Sisters in Crime.

Renée's website is **www.reneehorowitz.com**

Clocktower Books, San Diego

Clocktower Books, San Diego is a pioneering Web publisher of digital and print books. We began publishing full novels on the Web for download as early as 1996. Please visit our website at www.clocktowerbooks.com/.

Intriguing mystery novels
by Renée B. Horowitz
From Clocktower Books, San Diego:
ISBN: 1478149493

The Write Way To Murder
by Renée B. Horowitz

Marlene Dreyfus, an expert technical writer for a cutting-edge Phoenix aerospace firm, is drawn into a maelstrom of terror when her colleague Sam Garfield is found dead in a company hallway. Sam is covered in blood, with a huge knife sticking in his back.

Everyone is under suspicion as Security starts to investigate. Why was Sam Garfield killed? Was he involved in industrial espionage? Was he selling high tech secrets to foreign agents? Or had he uncovered the real perpetrator? Who will be next?

Marlene and her colleagues start looking over their shoulders—and at each other. Marlene is romantically interested in engineer Kevin Bronson—could he know more than he lets on? Assigned to replace Sam as project chief for a multi-million dollar proposal, Kevin has much to gain by Sam's death.

But suspects abound, and the clock is ticking. With so many baffling leads and dead ends, Marlene must find the killer before he (or she) strikes again.

Besides murder and love at work, Marlene has a home life to deal with. Daughters Fran and Cynthia add to Marlene's trials. Where did Bruce Underwood, Fran's fiancée, get the money for the mega-mansion he's building in Scottsdale? Why does Cynthia support her sister's former stalker?

Also by Rénee B. Horowitz:

The Rx Trilogy

In which acclaimed pharmacist sleuth & heroine Ruthie Kantor Morris, Registered Pharmacist Extraordinaire, solves cozies that will keep you awake all night, reading and wondering what happens next:

Book 1 of 3: Rx For Murder

What did his prescription records reveal to convince pharmacist Ruthie Kantor Morris that Harry Stokes's death was murder? As family members demand those records from Ruthie, suspicion shifts from the victim's young wife to the Scottsdale, Arizona pharmacist herself. Soon Ruthie finds she must unmask the murderer or become the next victim. An authentic behind-the-scenes look at pharmacy with a clever and charming heroine make this first novel in the Rx series a fascinating mystery of manners. (ISBN 978-0743312752)

Book 2 of 3: Deadly Rx

Did pharmacist Ruthie Kantor Morris make a fatal mistake in filling a teenage girl's prescription or did someone else substitute the blood-thinning medication? As Ruthie tries to prove that she didn't fill a deadly prescription, she finds herself in danger. (ISBN 9780743312776)

Book 3 of 3: Rx Alibi

When Andrea Felder is murdered, pharmacist Ruthie Kantor Morris discovers a prescription drug the police have overlooked. Does it pinpoint the killer or is it a false lead? Suspects include the Arizona pharmacist's best friend, Denise, and the mysterious Tony. (ISBN 0743312791)

www.ingramcontent.com/pod-product-compliance
Lightning Source LLC
Chambersburg PA
CBHW020948180626
46814CB00003B/985

* 9 780743 317290 *